CW00543479

TWIST IN TI

SHORT STORIES

VOLUME 3

A J BOOTHMAN

ALVASDA KEREZARD

TWIST IN THE TALE SHORT STORIES

Published by Alvasda Kerezard 2024

Copyright © A J Boothman, 2024

All rights reserved. No part of this book may be reproduced or used in any manner without written permission of the copyright owner except for the use of quotations in a book review.

This is a work of fiction. Names, characters, places and incidents are either the product of the author's imagination or used fictitiously. Any resemblance to actual persons, living or dead, events or locales is entirely coincidental.

ISBN 978-1-916537-40-8

CONTENTS

	PAGE
WHITE ARABIC	5
UNTIL DEATH DO US PART	29
A VALENTINE'S TALE	55
REFLECTIONS FROM A BRIDGE	73
CEDRIC AND THE VAMPIRES	83
THE ROOM	121
CEDRIC'S CHRISTMAS	133
A HALLOWEEN TALE	161
CEDRIC AND THE FORTUNE TELLER	175

WHITE

ARABIC

AUTHOR'S INTRODUCTION

I have written before about an idea for a story coming from a very ordinary occurrence, something innocuous that sparks an idea and develops into a hypothetical scenario. Such was the case with this tale.

A few months ago I went into the hall of my apartment and saw a package lying at the front door. It was in the familiar beige cardboard. I opened it to discover a pair of high heeled women's shoes. Clearly this was not meant for me, for one thing, I'm size 7 and these were only size 5.

I looked at the label on the packaging. The flat number was the same but it was for the block opposite and Miss Jones would be eagerly awaiting her new shoes. Being a good neighbour I took the package to her explaining that it had been delivered to me in error.

As I walked back I thought about the package. No doubt, like me, you have on occasion opened a parcel or letter meant for somebody else. In this case it was only a pair of shoes, but suppose it was something more significant.

The man in this story does exactly this only to discover that the contents of the package have deadly consequences.

WHITE ARABIC

Isaac Richards had not left his flat for ten years. Why would he? Everything he wanted could be got with the click of a button. The local supermarket delivered his shopping, take away meals were brought to him usually by a guy on a bike who was disgruntled at having to walk fifteen flights of stairs if the lift was not working and did not even get a tip. Everything else he required was delivered in a beige package. His entire social life took place through a large screen in the living room of his 15th storey flat in one of the twin tower blocks named Falcon and Kestrel which stood side by side in the Springburn area of Glasgow. Discoloured and flaking pictures of the birds were painted on the wall above the respective entrance doors. Although only an ornithologist would know the difference as the name plates had been destroyed by vandals years ago. His sitting room was stripped bare of furniture except for a large black leather armchair complete with recliner and raising footrest function, all operated by a remote control which was stored in a handy side pocket. The seat and armrests were showing signs of wear with small tears appearing. What can you expect if he spent virtually every waking moment of every day in it playing online games. He was able to eat his microwaved meals in it and had even slept in it on several occasions when he had been gaming deep into the night. What a great time to be alive.

Tonight was going to be a big night of gaming, a battle against an orc army. Everyone was really looking forward to it. He hoped Sergei the Slayer could make it, he had said he might have to work a nightshift. That was the great thing for Isaac, he never had to miss a session due to work, predominantly because he did not have a job. Sergei was from eastern Europe somewhere, that was another great thing, Isaac had friends from all over the world despite having met none of them, and not knowing their real names. Fair enough they did not know his either as he went by the name Thorbad the Destroyer, a huge muscular figure with a grizzled beard and long hair that streamed down over his armour carrying a great sword that he wielded in both hands. This image was in stark contrast to his own rather podgy, squat body with his squidgy face and bald head. It did not matter, he identified as Thorbad the Destroyer, this was the persona he saw himself as every day, this is how all his online friends knew him.

Pizza had been delivered earlier in the evening which he had scoffed and dispatched the empty box down the rubbish chute in the kitchen, a saving grace which avoided trips down to the bins on the ground floor.

Soon he was engrossed in the game. The screen flashed with colour and the surround sound created a wall of noise around him as explosions and shouts filled the room. He slashed his way through orcs as the battle raged, so emersed was he that he did not hear the knock on his door or the sound of a package landing on the hall floor.

Sun light was just breaking through his curtains when he awoke slumped in the armchair. He looked around through bleary eyes, the screen was still on displaying a still frame from the game. Groggily he pushed himself up and ambled out into the hall. Near the front door he noticed the slim beige package on the floor. He could not recollect ordering anything, he thought, as he bent down and picked it up, squinting at the name. Mr. I. Richard. This was something that really annoyed him, people getting his name wrong, it was Richards, not Richard. He turned the package and looked at the shape wondering what it was. A book? About the right size but probably a bit too heavy. He ripped open the cardboard to find the package full of small polystyrene balls. What could it be, he wondered? He reached into the balls and felt something hard and rectangular. The polystyrene balls fell to the ground along with a folded sheet of paper as he pulled it out. Almost in slow motion the cardboard dropped to the floor with a thud as he stared open mouthed at the cellophane wrapped around the fine white powder. Slowly he traipsed into the kitchen, his eyes never wavering from the package held out in front of him. Inside the kitchen the curtains were open and he could see Kestrel tower. He quickly put the package behind his back and closed them. This needed to be done in absolute secret, the last thing he wanted was to be seen. He had heard you can test it by rubbing it on your gums, although there seemed little doubt as to what it was. Carefully he cut a small hole in the corner and dipped the tip of his little finger into the powder. His gums tingled as he applied it. He placed it on the counter and went into the hall. The floor was covered in small white polystyrene balls and torn beige cardboard. Against the skirting board he saw the folded paper. He knelt down and opened it. At the top in black capital letters were the words "WHITE ARABIC." His hands trembled and his mind raced, What was he going to do? This was a large quantity of drugs, clearly not for private use, this was for a dealer, a gangster. He picked up the torn cardboard that had the address and read.

Mr. I. Richard, 15/1 Kestrel Tower

It had been delivered to the wrong address, whoever had delivered it had mistaken Falcon Tower for Kestrel Tower. It explained the name too. This I. Richard was clearly a dealer. What should he do? His first thought was to deliver it himself. How could he explain that the package was opened. This guy was very probably a dangerous criminal. It would not auger well for him showing up with an open drugs package. What was White Arabic anyway? He did not know that much about the world of drugs and had certainly never heard of White Arabic. It looked like cocaine to him. He could not take the package to Kestrel Tower in this state. At the same time he did not want to be discovered with it himself, that would bode even more ominously. He would need to get rid of the evidence. The cardboard and polystyrene could be thrown down the rubbish chute. He went into the kitchen and returned with a black bin liner, quickly scooping up all the polystyrene and cardboard up. Back in the kitchen he filled the sink with water and peeled the address label from the package. He submerged it in the water along with the delivery note until the paper softened then rolled them into a mush. No-one would be able to read them now. He threw them into the bin liner and looked at the White Arabic on the counter. That could not very well be thrown that down the chute, it would need to be disposed of separately. He tied the top of the bin liner securely and tossed it down. It made a swooshing sound as it descended to the bins below. Now for the drugs. He picked up the package and went into the bathroom. This would be an end of the matter, nobody would be able to trace it back to him. He lifted the toilet seat and paused. This was a lot of drugs, how much was it worth? It could not hurt to find out before he got rid of it.

He opened a drawer and placed the digital scales on the counter before putting the package on. The weight appeared on the screen, 1 kilogram exactly. He went into the living room and sat down on the edge of the armchair using his keyboard to search the internet on his television. No results for White Arabic. Perhaps this was something new and as yet unknown he thought. He did a new search on cocaine. The data appeared; UK street value for cocaine £40,000 per kilogram. His eyes opened wide and his heart raced, £40.000, he was sitting on £40,000. But how could he sell it? He did not want to stand around on street corners. Online? Yes, he had it, in the virtual world he was anonymous. And he knew just the place.

****

"Where's the package/"

"You should have it, Ivan. It was despatched three days ago."

"Well, I don't. You'd better not be trying to double cross me."

His knuckles were white as he tightened his grip on the phone and paced up and down the flat.

"It was sent to the usual address, 15/1 Kestrel Tower."

"Turn that off, Tommy!" he yelled at the scrawny man sat playing the video game. He turned the sound off as on the television screen warriors and orcs fought in a medieval setting.

"You should have got it yesterday."

"Look, it's not arrived, has it. I'm a dangerous man to mess with."

"So are we, Mr. Richard."

The line went dead.

****

Isaac sat in his armchair with his mic strapped to his head and remote control in hand. On the television screen Thorbad walked slowly along the dimly lit street, graffiti covered the walls and a burnt out car was crashed into a lamp post. The windows of the surrounding buildings were boarded up with wooden planks, all except one. A neon sign flickered above a black metal door, "The Black Dragon." He pushed the door and entered the dusky bar. Torches burnt on the brick walls providing some illumination. He approached the bar and looked around. Behind the bar a goblin was serving drinks to a dwarf. At a corner table sat three trolls drinking from large metal tankards.

"You buying or selling?"

Towering above him was a Tauren Warrior, his horns jutting out horizontally just above his shoulders before tilting upwards into sharp points. His bull like face was hard with a metal ring through the nose and braided hair hanging down both sides to his chest. Strapped to his back was a large double bladed axe.

"Selling." spluttered Isaac hesitantly.

"Yea, what?"

Isaac could feel his mouth dry as he looked around the bar furtively.

"White Arabic," he whispered, his mouth dry.

"What's that?"

Isaac paused and thought, what actually was it? The Tauren Warrior was waiting for his reply.

11

"It's a bit like cocaine."

"A bit like cocaine?"

Isaac could sense his scepticism, he had to say something else.."

"Engineered cocaine," he said finally.

The Tauren Warrior was silent. On the screen he was motionless. Maybe this was a bad idea, he thought as panic set in. What did he know about selling drugs, not to mention the illegality. He was engaging in criminal activity, still it was a lot of money and no-one knew who he was or where he lived.

"How much for 2 grams?"

If 1 kilogram was worth £40,000, thought Isaac, then 2 grams should be,,,

"£80."

Was this actually going to happen, he thought as he waited for a response.

"Ok."

Isaac could feel his heart rate increase.

"How do you want to do this?" he asked.

"Put it in the post and I'll send you the money when I receive it."

Isaac thought quickly, could he trust this person to pay. Plus he was not keen to give out his address, that would allow someone to identify him.

"Well?"

Or he could set up a PO Box. That would take a bit of time and this guy was waiting for a response.

"I do not want to give out my address?"

"I'll put the money into your account."

Isaac was not keen to do that either. What if he was a scammer? Not that there was much money in the account. He had to do something before this guy lost interest. He decided to take the risk.

"Ok but put the money in the account first."

"No way, I've been ripped off like that before."

Isaac was unsure how to proceed. If he sent the stuff he may never hear from this guy again, on the other hand he had come by it by chance anyway so what was he really losing.

"Look, if it's good I'll buy more from you, I've been looking for new gear for a while."

Isaac decided to trust him. He got the address and gave out his account details before coming off line and going into the kitchen.

He searched the cupboards for something to package the drugs in. At the back of the one under the sink he found a roll of kitchen foil covered in dust that he had bought optimistically years earlier with the intention of cooking more but had actually only used once. Perfect, he thought, as he placed it on the counter and carefully cut a small square with the scissors. He put in on top of the scales and smoothed it out before switching the scales on and setting the digital weight display to zero. In the drawer he took out a small teaspoon and very delicately started to put the white powder on top of the foil. His heart was beating fast as he thought about what he was doing, so nervous and excited that he struggled to keep his hand still as he put more and more onto the scales, vigilantly watching the display. 1.8 grams, 1.9 grams. He dipped the spoon into the powder one last time and gingerly shook it above the foil sprinkling it gently, his eyes focused on the unchanging display. The powder floated down as he shook the spoon a little bit more. The numbers changed, 2 grams. Isaac let out a huge sigh of relief and added the remnants on the spoon back to the package. He gripped the edges of the foil lightly and carefully folded the sides over the powder horizontally and vertically until it was securely encased. Finally he smoothed it down with his palms until it was flat. So far, so good. He was going to need an envelope.

As he left the building he felt the warm sun on his face, something he had not experienced in over ten years of voluntary solitude. He walked between the two towers to a small shop. Outside on the pavement was a metal newspaper board. Isaac stopped and read the headline, *Glasgow drug problem increases.* He looked through the window at the eclectic mix of goods: tools, light bulbs, detergent bottles, tinned food, newspapers. This was the only shop on the estate and it provided everything to everybody. An old woman came out through the door wheeling a trolley behind her full of dog food. He watched as she trundled away and disappeared from view. The street was quiet, Isaac looked at the closed door then furtively glanced left and right. He took a deep breath, steeled himself and went in.

Inside it seemed the only person was a young lad slumped behind the counter reading the sports pages of a newspaper. That suited Isaac, he wanted to get in and out with as little attention as possible. He looked around the store. The aisles were tall and narrow, crammed with products, the envelopes could be absolutely anywhere, there were no signs, this was a far cry from a major supermarket. There was no other choice than to search. He snaked his way up and down the aisles, his eyes scanning every shelf. Finally at the very end of the very last aisle he found a rack stacked with envelopes of different sizes and colours. As he looked at the display he thought about the size of the tin foil package in his flat, there was no way he was going to bring it with him, he was anxious enough having it at all. There were no prices on any of the envelopes, he did not want to spend any more than was necessary. The smaller envelopes would probably be cheaper, he reasoned. He picked up a slim brown one, it looked about the right size. Suddenly, the door opened, banging against the side wall, making him jump and dropping the envelope.

""I'm not paying you to sit on your arse, get those shelves stacked," said the old man who entered in a gruff voice.

The youth loped lazily from behind the counter and disappeared down one of the aisles. Isaac bent down and retrieved the envelope as the old man settled in behind the counter. He moved cautiously down the aisle until he reached him, placing the envelope on the counter.

"Anything else?"

"Do you have a stamp/"

"First or second class?"

"Second."

The old man placed a booklet on the counter.

"I only need one."

"They come in booklets of twelve, if you want a single stamp you will need to go to the post office."

"No, that's fine," said Isaac hurriedly. "I'll take the booklet."

"£10."

"£10 for an envelope and twelve stamps!"

"Second class stamps have gone up to 75p now."

"Fine, " replied Isaac giving him a £10 note.

He shoved the envelope and stamps into his pocket out of sight. £10, he thought, as he hurried back to his flat, that would eat into his profits, or even worse, be money lost if he did not get paid.

Back in the flat he wrote the address on the envelope and slipped the tin foil package inside. He went back out to the post box just outside the tower. A quick look around and he whipped it out of his pocket and dropped it in. The deed was done all he could now was wait.

"£50,000. I'm down £50.000," raged Ivan Richard.

The passing days had not mellowed his anger.

"I thought you only paid £10.000," replied Tommy as he sat cross-legged on the floor in front of the screen, feverishly pressing the buttons on the console in his hands.

"I could have sold it for £50, 000. Those English bastards have ripped me off. I knew I should never have trusted them."

"Why would they suddenly do that? They have made the delivery every time until now."

"Greed, pure greed, probably got a better offer elsewhere and just kept my cash."

Ivan stood behind Tommy and looked at his character on the screen, a tall, slim elf with a thin face and pointed ears and nose, in fact, he did not look much different to Tommy himself. The elf went into a dingy, dimly lit bar full of other weird creatures: trolls, goblins, orcs. It never ceased to amaze Ivan that grown men would waste their time on a child's game. Suddenly a voluptuous female warrior appeared, her long black hair cascaded around her armour which barley covered her large breasts and exposed her deep cleavage. Leather straps covered her wrists and the tattoo of a coiled cobra was visible on her muscular upper arm. Between her short skirt and knee high lace up boots her toned thighs were revealed. Her face had an angelic beauty with her soft contours and pale complexion, but her dark piercing eyes and captivating scarlet lips expressed a hidden danger that lurked within.

"I see why you play the game now," observed Ivan.

"Don't be fooled by appearances," replied Tommy.

"What do you mean?"

"Could be a man. You can be anyone you want to be on here."

The name Aello appeared above her.

"Strange name," said Ivan.

"It's the name of one of the harpies from Greek mythology."

"What the hell's a harpy?"

16

"They were three winged sisters who had the faces of beautiful maidens but hearts of evil. They moved swiftly and silently abducting people to take to their lair to torture and finally kill. Actually a very appropriate name."

"Why's that?"

"I've heard a few rumours that she makes people disappear in the outside world,. If you want someone taken care of she can arrange it, for the right price."

"Whatever, we need to solve this problem, you're not going to find White Arabic in The Black Dragon."

Where was the money? Isaac checked his account online yet again. Several days had passed and he had received nothing. He went into the kitchen to make a cup of tea. That guy was not going to pay him, he knew it all along. He had been scammed. But what could he do? He could not go to the police. What would he say, excuse me, but someone has not paid me for the drugs I sent them. He might as well just walk into the local station, stretch out his hands and ask them to slap the cuffs on him.. And another thing, what was he supposed to do with the rest of the drugs? He could flush it down the toilet, he supposed, he had seen that done in films. Then again that would literally be throwing money down the pan. That idea did not sit well with him, at all. £40.000! Maybe he could contact his bank. No, that would alert them to his activities, they no doubt had a fraud and criminal investigation department.

He returned to the sitting room and looked at his account on screen. Suddenly he sat bolt upright, his eyes open wide, there it was, a new entry, £80. A broad smile spread across his face.

That night he was back in The Black Dragon. This was an incredibly easy way to make money, perhaps there would be others he could sell to. He sat at the bar and surveyed the room. There were plenty of orcs, trolls and druids. At the end of the bar he could see

Aello talking to a warlock. He had seen her about in the game but never actually engaged with her. Being in a virtual world did not make it any easier for him to talk to girls.

"I hoped you'd be here," said a voice behind him.

It was the Tauren Warrior.

"That White Arabic is good stuff, got any more?"

"Yea, how much do you want?"

"I'll take 5 grams this time."

"£200."

"I'll put the money in your account after delivery like before."

The Tauren Warrior moved away.

This was fantastic, £200 for just posting a letter. He would need more envelopes, perhaps he would buy a bundle, and more stamps, save him constant trips to the shop. He was going to be rich. He felt great, this was so easy. Aello moved passed him.

"Hi," he said daringly, emboldened by his success.

She completely ignored him and disappeared through the door.

Isaac looked at his account on the screen, over £10.000, it had never been so high. After only two weeks word had got out and he only needed to go into The Black Dragon and he was being approached by druids, warlocks and orcs. He did not know a lot about drugs but this White Arabic was clearly good stuff. Orders were coming in daily. He had decided to buy stamps and envelopes online to avoid any suspicion about his activities. Things were going great and going to stay that way.

The elf stood at the end of the bar in The Black Dragon, the place was quiet, only a few warlocks sat in the corner. Aello entered, her dark hair swaying behind her as she moved. The elf looked at her voluptuous figure and taut bare thighs.

"You buying or selling?"

A warlock with a purple cloak and long white beard had approached him.

"Neither." replied the elf ogling Aello's ample bosom and exposed cleavage.

"Have you seen a warrior in here goes by the name of Thorbad?"

"No."

"He has some great gear."

"Good for him," said the elf testily.

"I'd never heard of it before."

The elf began to move away from the irritating warlock and towards Aello.

"It's called White Arabic."

The elf stopped dead.

"What is it called?" he asked turning.

"White Arabic."

"Who did you say you got it from?"

"A warrior goes by the name Thorbad."

"And you bought it in here?"

"That's right, amazing stuff, I'm hoping I can get some more tonight."

Suddenly the elf disappeared.

High up in the tower block Tommy sat before the screen. He had found their White Arabic.

Isaac had become a bit of a cottage industry, weighing the White Arabic, wrapping it in the foil, and posting it to his customers. The supply was decreasing and he had no idea how to get more. Still he could enjoy his good fortune while it lasted.

"I want him dead!" shouted Ivan slamming his fist on the table. "Let me get on that game."

"Easy, Ivan," placated Tommy. "If you go in with all guns blazing he will depart the game and we will lose him. Let me talk to him."

"What good will talking do?"

"I can find out who he is and where he lives."

"Ok but be quick about it."

Isaac was back on the game, his character Thorbad was in The Black Dragon looking for more business. The bar was busy, he would not have to wait long, his reputation was growing quickly.

"I hear your selling White Arabic."

Isaac smiled, his first sale of the night was on the way. He turned and looked at the tall, thin elf.

"That's right, how much do you want?"

"That accent, he's Scottish," said Ivan sat beside Tommy and listening eagerly.

"One gram."

"£40."

"And he's under cutting our price," exclaimed Ivan.

"Ok. Can we meet in the real world," asked the elf.

"No. I'll post it and you can put the money into my account."

The elf fell silent.

"We need to find out who he is," said Ivan.

"If we do what he asks we will have his bank account details to identify him."

"No, that's no good, banks will not give out that sort of information."

"Ok, but at least the post mark on the letter will tell us which town he's in."

"Ok, do it, but have the package delivered to your address in Forest Street."

****

"It's here," said Tommy entering Ivan's flat with the envelope in hand.

Ivan took it from him and they went into the kitchen. He placed it on the counter and sliced it open with a knife. The sun glistened off the silver foil. Ivan carefully unfolded it until he could see the white powder. He dipped his finger into it and put it on his tongue.

"Its White Arabic," he proclaimed. "What's the postmark?"

Tommy picked up the envelope.

"It's Glasgow."

"So, he's near. We need to arrange to meet and deal with this guy."

"That could be tricky, he seems afraid to meet."

"Tempt him with a large order."

"Like what?"

"100 grams should draw him out, then we'll deal with him."

The elf was back in The Black Dragon. He found Thorbad standing alone at the bar.

"I hoped I'd find you here," he said approaching.

"You looking to get some more."

"Yea, 100 grams."

Isaac could not believe his ears, 100 grams, £4,000. This would be his biggest deal by some distance.

"I can supply that," he said eagerly.

It suddenly crossed his mind that it could be a scam. What if this person got the 100 grams then disappeared without ever paying him. He had been fortunate up to now, but that had only been a few grams each time.

"This time I want £2,000 paid before delivery and £2,000 after," he added.

"Don't you trust me?"

"It's not that, it's just that it's rather a lot of money."

"I've got a better idea, we can meet in person. You're in Glasgow, aren't you?"

Isaac sat bolt upright, stunned and nervous.

"How do you know where I live?"

"The postmark on the envelope was Glasgow."

Isaac had not considered the postmark, clearly everyone he had sent packages to knew he was in Glasgow. Although, it was a big place, no one knew exactly where he reassured himself. Still, it was enough information to be too close for comfort.

"I don't want to meet, I prefer to post. Just put half in my account and I will send the package, then put in the other half."

Ivan was clenching his teeth, his impatience growing.

"No. it's too much money. Either we meet or no deal."

Isaac thought, he was keen to get £4,000 but not to meet. What could he do?

"I'm not keen."

"Where do you live?" demanded Ivan ripping the mic violently off Tommy's head.

"Who's that?" said Isaac startled at hearing this gruff and threatening new voice. "Is someone there with you?"

"You little weasel, do you know who I am?" shouted Ivan menacingly. "I want my gear back."

"You're going to scare him away," said Tommy trying to get the head mic back but being pushed away roughly by Ivan.

On the screen Thorbad has disappeared.

"I told you, Ivan, now we've lost him," said Tommy.

"Get him back."

"How?"

"I don't know. You're the expert."

"There may be another way, but it will cost you."

"I don't care what it costs, I want him taken care of."

Isaac huddled up on his chair shaking, the real dealer had found him.

****

Aello sat in a dark corner of The Black Dragon, the candle on the table casting her silhouette on the brick wall behind. Her sword was placed beside the candle, the sharp blade pointing forward and the leather bound handle close enough to be grabbed at any moment and wielded with deadly power. The elf approached.

"I am in need of your services on the outside world," he said.

"She pushed back a chair with her boot and he sat.

"I need someone taken care of," he whispered.

"£20,000, half before the job and half after," she replied in a husky voice.

"Fine."

"Who is the mark?"

"A warrior goes by the name of Thorbad."

"I've seen him around."

"There's one other thing. He has some white powder belonging to us, we want it back."

"White Arabic."

"How do you know about it?" he asked surprised.

"I've heard it talked about in here. I'll let you know when the job is complete."

The elf got up and left.

Isaac had not been back to The Black Dragon in over a week. That encounter with the elf had really scared him. The real dealers were out there looking for him. Yet he still had over half of the White Arabic remaining, £20,000. The pull was too strong to resist.

On screen he entered the seedy bar. It seemed even darker than usual.

"I haven't seen you in here for a while?" said a soft voice behind him.

He turned, surprised to see it was Aello, her jet black hair cascading around her strikingly beautiful face and her scantily clad body exposing her tantalisingly bare flesh.

"No, I-I've been busy," replied Isaac stumbling over his words.

"I just wanted to apologise for ignoring you before, I was having a bad day."

"Oh, no problem, I know what that's like."

"Why, are you having a bad day?"

"A bad week, that's why I've not been on the game recently."

"I get lonely, even though I live in a big city."

"Which city?"

"I'm not sure I should tell you, there are a few weirdos on here."

"I'm not a weirdo," protested Isaac.

"Alright, I'll tell you if you tell me where you are."

"Ok."

Glasgow."

"I live in Glasgow too," said Isaac excitedly.

"Where about?"

"I don't like to say."

"Do you look like your character?" asked Aello changing tack.

"Well, no," admitted Isaac slightly embarrassed.

"Doesn't matter, you seem nice."

"Do you look like your character?"

"Pretty much, I have long black hair and an hour glass figure."

Isaac looked at her on screen, she was stunning.

"If you were close by we could meet." she said seductively., "Whereabouts?"

Isaac had not known many women and none in over ten years. Who knew how many more chances he would get. Of course, she could be lying, or if they met she might not fancy him. He decided to take the chance.

"Springburn."

Aello brought up a map of the area on her screen.

"I know it. Do you live by yourself?"

"Yes, I have a flat."

"I could visit you on the weekend, would you like that."

"Yes, I would," he replied eagerly.

This could actually happen he thought elatedly.

"What's your address?"

"Falcon Tower, flat 15/1."

"Great, how about Saturday night 10pm?"

"Yes, fantastic."

"Ok, I have to go now. Until Saturday."

Isaac was ecstatic, a woman was interested in him, and not just an ordinary woman but a stunningly beautiful one. She said she looked like her character, he would have to order some after shave online.

Aello switched the map to a street view of Falcon Tower. It looked simple enough although Glasgow was a long drive. She reached into the drawer and removed the silenced pistol.

Isaac looked at his watch yet again as he looked through the window down through the darkness at the court in front of the tower. Midnight and nothing was moving outside, he knew it was too good to be true, Aello should have been here two hours ago. He had even gone online and into The Black Dragon but she was not there. He closed the curtains and dejectedly went into the bedroom putting on his pyjamas before turning out the light and slipping between the sheets.

It was almost three hours later when a car pulled up across the street from the towers. The door opened silently and a figure dressed in black stepped out, the hood pulled up over the head. They walked quickly across the deserted court to the tower. Outside the entrance they stopped and looked at the bird painted on the wall. Its eyes were piercing and its beak was curved into a sharp point. They removed a small box from their pocket and attached it to the electronic lock. Digital numbers appeared on the display and the lock clicked. They removed the device and went inside. The foyer was dimly illuminated by a single flickering bulb at the rear. The figure approached the lifts and pressed the button with a gloved hand. The doors opened immediately and they stepped in. As the lift ascended they removed the silenced pistol from inside their jacket. They took out the magazine, examined it. The light glinted off the bullets. They reinserted it snapping it securely in place and concealed it back inside their jacket. The lift doors opened and they stepped stealthily into the corridor. Floor 15. All was quiet. They moved along the passage to the end, flat 15/1. The door was discoloured with the brown paint flaking around the edges. They knelt down and inserted a pick into the lock. It made a light scratching sounds as it was delicately manoeuvred. They stood up, put it away and lowered a gloved hand gently onto the handle. Slowly and silently they turned it and eased the door open. As they entered into the pitch black hall they pulled out the pistol. Behind one of the doors they could hear light snoring. They tightened their grip on the gun and placed their finger lightly on the trigger. The figure put their hand on the knob and twisted it gradually. Suddenly the snoring stopped, they stood still, waiting and listening. For a moment all was quiet then the snoring resumed. The door inched open and they entered the sark room. In the bed they could see the outline of the slumbering person. They drew near and pointed the barrel at the head. Their finger tensed on the trigger. A sound like rushing wind filled the air followed by another. Blood seeped across the pillow. The figure moved swiftly away and was gone.

As the sun rose, outside the local shop there was a new headline on the newspaper board, *Drug dealer Ivan Richard shot dead last night.*

UNTIL DEATH DO US PART

AUTHOR'S INTRODUCTION

The first of four stories in this book featuring thirtysomething socialites Cedric and Penelope. Cedric has a wild imagination that is counter balanced by the grounded rationality of Penelope but sometimes even she cannot help but get caught up in his outrageous ideas.

These tales are a bit different from the others, being almost written in the form of a play. It is structured in acts and scenes and mostly dialogue, however, as you will see, it does not adhere to the traditional play format.

The stories have a strong comedic element while still maintaining the dramatic and unexpected endings.

Characters

Elizabeth, The Bride

Robert, The Groom

Cedric, Friend of Elizabeth, Penelope's husband

Penelope, Friend of Elizabeth, Cedric's wife

Jack, The Best Man

Lady Thorndyke, a rich aristocrat

Sir Donald, Elizabeth's father

ACT I

SCENE 1

A CHURCH IN ENGLAND

THE WEDDING

"Dearly beloved, we are gathered here today to join this man, Robert Spratt, and this woman, Elizabeth Cavendish-Leveson, in holy matrimony."

"Betty Spratt. I bet that will go down well at the country club. I can just see it now, "Lady Thorndyke, may I present Bob and Betty Spratt.""

"Shhh, Cedric," rebuked Penelope. "They might hear you."

"What, right back here? I can barely see them through that whopping great hat in front."

The old woman in the hat turned her head and gave him a stern, disapproving look.

"Good afternoon, Lady Thorndyke," said Cedric cheerily. "Love the hat."

She snorted derisively and turned her head haughtily back to the front.

"That's another Christmas card list we're off, Penelope," he whispered.

"Do you think she should be getting married in white?"

"Why not, probably the same dress as the previous two times, may as well get her money's worth out of it."

"It's not the same dress, you are awful, Cedric."

"It always baffles me why women spend so much money on a dress they are only going to wear once, I think Miss Havisham had the right idea."

"Hmm."

" I always wear the same morning suit."

"That's different, you only have one morning suit. And it's beginning to fade."

"No-one's looking at me, the bride is always the centre of attention. In Lizzie's case for the third time."

"I hope she has better luck this time."

"I hope he has better luck."

"What are you implying, Cedric?"

"You know very well what I'm implying. Penelope."

"Her previous husbands died in tragic accidents."

"That's debateable, their bodies were never found, they completely disappeared, never to be seen again. She is like the Bermuda Triangle for husbands. Probably buried in her garden."

"That's a terrible thing to say, Cedric."

"All I'm saying is her rhubarb always comes up nice."

"I Elizabeth Cavendish-Leveson, take you Robert Spratt to be my husband...."

"Third."

"Shhh, Cedric."

"...to have and to hold from this day forward, for better, for worse, for richer, for poorer..."

"For richer."

"Cedric!"

"...to love and to cherish, until death do us part."

Penelope glared at Cedric.

"I didn't say anything," he protested.

"You were thinking it."

"I was thinking about the reception."

"You needn't think you're getting drunk again."

"I don't get drunk," objected Cedric.

"At the last one you threw up in the Rhododendrons."

"That was the oysters."

"Hmm," mused Penelope sceptically as the bride and groom made their way back down the aisle.

"Thank heavens it's over," complained Cedric getting up. "You'd think they would make these pews more comfortable."

"It is a church, Cedric,"

"I'm bringing a cushion next time, my arse is killing me. Sorry, Lady Thorndyke, I mean, I am experiencing a slight discomfort in my nether regions."

"Stop saying things to upset her, you know how sensitive she is," admonished Penelope as Lady Thorndyke marched loftily down the aisle. "She still hasn't got over the vomit on her Rhododendrons."

SCENE 2

A LUXURY 5 STAR HOTEL

THE RECEPTION

"Raise your glasses with me and toast the happy couple. To Elizabeth and Robert."

"TO ELIZABETH AND ROBERT!"

"He must know that speech by heart by now. He's delivered it enough times."

"Shhh, Cedric. Robert is about to speak.

A small, mousy man got timidly to his feet, beads of perspiration visible on the ample forehead below his thin, receding hair. He adjusted his thick spectacles and looked with some trepidation at the expectant faces before him.

"Th-thank you, Sir Donald. I-I must admit that after forty years I had almost given up hope of marriage. And indeed it was something of a surprise when Elizabeth approached me at Lady Thorndyke's garden fête a few months ago. My company was providing the sandwiches and I was only there to check up on things. Most people have no interest when I tell them I make and sell sandwiches for a living, but Elizabeth was engrossed in my business."

"And the money you make," whispered Cedric refilling his glass from the magnum of champagne on the table.

"It has been something of a whirlwind romance but I am delighted and looking forward to spending the rest of my life with Elizabeth."

"Which might be shorter than you think."

"Shhh, Cedric."

"To Elizabeth."

"TO ELIZABETH!"

He sat down wiping the sweat from his brow and sighing with relief before taking a quick sip from his flute.

"Well, well, who'd have thought it, old Bob finally getting married," said the tall, firm jawed man next to him rising assuredly to his feet. "I was beginning to think he would have to leave his fortune to the dogs' home. It must be over twenty years since I have seen Bob and I must confess I was surprised to get a phone call out of the blue asking me to be best man. I guess, you still haven't got around to reading *How To Win Friends and Influence People*, Bob. Even more surprised that Bob built up a fortune making sandwiches and selling them around the office blocks. Don't get me wrong, at school we all had Bob pegged for a career in sandwiches, but we thought it was more likely to be serving Big Macs. I'm given to believe that he put in a bid to provide the sandwiches for this reception but was unsuccessful. On the plus side no one will go home with stomach cramps and spend the night on the toilet.

But credit where credit is due, Bob did make his way in the world and is now married. The only thing I would say to Elizabeth is, having seen Bob dance, I hope you brought some hobnail boots for the first waltz. To Bob, or now that he's moving into society, I should say Robert. To Robert and Elizabeth."

"TO ROBERT AND ELIZABETH!"

(Later in the evening)

"That's enough dancing for now, Penelope," panted Cedric staggering wearily from the dance floor. "I'm getting a drink."

"I'll come with you."

"Look, there's that best man stood at the bar. Let's introduce ourselves."

"You just want to grill him about Robert."

"Come on."

They weaved their way through the crowd to the bar.

"Very nice speech, I'm Cedric Harrington and this is my wife, Penelope,"

"Jack Thomson," he slurred looking through bleary eyes as he knocked back a glass of whisky.

"So, you are an old school chum of Robert?"

"Don't know if chum is the right word but I was certainly at school with Bob. In fact, I hadn't seen him since school. I was amazed when he asked me to be best man. I guess he hasn't got any friends, same in school really."

"No. I didn't notice any here, nor family."

"No, he has no family. He was brought up in an orphanage," said Jack tilting his head back and emptying the remaining whisky into his mouth.

"That's very sad," said Penelope sympathetically.

"Another whisky, barman," yelled Jack loudly waving his empty glass in his direction.

"Good news for Liz," murmured Cedric. "Nobody to be suspicious when he disappears."

"Still, he's done very well for himself," said Penelope elbowing him in the ribs.

Jack's entire attention was on the barman as he refilled his glass.

"I was just saying," repeated Penelope. "He's done well for himself and now he has Elizabeth."

"Oh, yes, I suppose so. I believe she's a widow?"

"Yes, that's right."

"Twice," said Cedric guarding his ribs with his arms.

"Twice!"

"Yes, first she was married to Charlie Fletcher, partner in the Redmond Fletcher Quarry," elaborated Cedric.

"What happened to him?"

"They had set up some explosives to break some of the rock and he went to check one night and was blown up. All they found of him was his boots, still smouldering."

"Good, God! What happened to the second one?"

"That was Tommy Tibbs, ran a plumbing company. He went fishing in his rowing boat one night and was never seen again. They found his boat adrift on the lake."

"That's terrible."

"Not for Lizzie, she inherited two fortunes."

"So, she's rich then?"

"Well, she was."

"She was?"

"She has spent most of it. Let's just say she has expensive tastes. Just look at their honeymoon, two weeks in Dubai. Then there is the annual ski trips to St. Moritz, the yacht parties, the country club…"

"I'm sure Jack is not interested in all that," interrupted Penelope.

"Just as well old Bob has money then," said Jack polishing off the whisky.

"Indeed."

"Oh. Look they're leaving, Let's see them off," said Penelope taking Cedric's arm and dragging him outside.

The couple were getting into the back of the limousine.

"Have a lovely time, Lizzie," shouted Penelope. "See you when you come back. And you too, Robert."

"We hope," said Cedric.

ACT II

SCENE 1

ELIZABETH'S HOUSE

TWO WEEKS LATER

"Come in and take a seat," welcomed Elizabeth showing Cedric and Penelope into the lounge.

"You're looking very tanned, Lizzie," observed Penelope.

"The weather is always wonderful in Dubai."

"Where's Robert?" enquired Cedric wondering if he had in fact made it back.

"He's getting some wine, makes it himself, you know."

"Did you have a nice time?" asked Penelope.

"Simply delightful, you must see all the photographs we took. I put them into an album. Wait here and I'll go and get it," said Elizabeth leaving the room.

"Be something to remember him by when he's gone."

"Now stop that Cedric," rebuked Penelope.

The door opened and Robert entered carrying a tray.

"What happened to you?" exclaimed Cedric staring at the brace around his neck.

"I was involved in a car crash in Dubai."

"Are you alright?" asked Penelope concerned.

"Just a slight whiplash, I should be able to take it off tomorrow."

"Just as well," said Elizabeth coming back in with a bulging photo album. "Remember you have to fix those broken tiles on the roof and we are visiting Lady Thorndyke for lunch tomorrow. Best if you are not wearing the brace, she is very sensitive to reminders of death and infirmity, given her age."

"Tell us about your crash," said Cedric eagerly.

"It was the funniest thing. We hired a car and Elizabeth asked me to go out one night to get some tablets for a headache. Well, I went out and the brakes failed. They had been fine that morning when Elizabeth had gone to the hairdresser's. Anyway, I crashed into a tree and was taken to hospital. Fortunately, my only injury was a bit of a stiff neck, so they gave me the brace to wear."

"How terrible, and on your honeymoon too. You had a lucky escape, Robert," empathised Penelope.

"The second."

"The second?" spluttered Cedric almost choking on his wine.

"Yes, only a few days earlier. I was going scuba diving. We were on the boat and while I was putting on my wetsuit Elizabeth kindly brought me the oxygen tank. I'm quite an experienced diver so I went down in the water while the instructor was helping another diver get ready on the boat. I was diving deeper and deeper when the tube got detached from the nozzle on the oxygen tank. As the air gushed out I scrambled to reattach it but it was too awkward reaching behind me. Fortunately, I have always had big lungs so I was just about able to make my way back to the surface before I ran out of breath."

"Gosh!" exclaimed Penelope. "Another close call."

"Yes, I've never known the tube to come off before. I don't know how it happened."

"You are so accident prone, Robert," said Elizabeth serenely, sipping her wine.

"I seem to be. It's funny though, I never used to be."

SCENE 2

CEDRIC AND PENELOPE'S HOUSE

THE FOLLOWING DAY

"I tell you she's trying to kill him, Penelope."

"Are you still going on about that, Cedric. I told you it's utter nonsense."

"How do you explain the brakes failing on the car?"

"These things do happen, you know."

"But Lizzie had been driving the car that morning and they were fine. And what about the tube coming off the Scuba tank."

"Must have not been checked properly by the instructor."

"He said Lizzie had got the tank for him. She could have tampered with the tube."

"In front of everyone on the boat?"

"We don't know where she got it from. Perhaps she was alone in a storeroom."

"Why don't you ring Robert and ask him?"

"Good idea," said Cedric picking up the phone.

"Don't you dare, Cedric. I was only joking. All these ideas of Lizzie trying to bump him off are in your head."

"What about the others?" said Cedric, reluctantly putting down the phone.

"What others?"

"The other husbands, Charlie Fletcher and Tommy Tibbs?"

"Are you still on about that. They died in freak accidents."

"I'm not so sure, their bodies were never found, and Lizzie did very well financially."

"If Lizzie has all their money why would she need Robert's?"

"She has spent it all, she could not even afford to get the roof tiles repaired. That house is all she has, though it's probably worth a pretty penny."

"So, according to you what has she done with their bodies?"

"Buried them in the garden. Right after both men were supposedly killed in accidents new flowerbeds appeared."

"Why didn't the police dig them up then?"

"Because of Lady Thorndyke."

"Lady Thorndyke?"

"You know how close Lizzie is to Lady Thorndyke. She treats Lizzie like a favourite niece. Plus she has so much influence in the community that the police would not dare to dig up the garden."

"So, where does that leave us?"

"Waiting for Robert to vanish and a new flowerbed to appear."

"Hmm."

"Unless we stop her."

"And how do you to propose to do that?"

"By digging up the flowerbeds and discovering the bodies."

"How are you going to do that?"

"Let me think. she said they are going to visit Lady Thorndyke for lunch today. They will probably be there for hours going through that photo album as Lizzie will insist on telling a story about virtually every snap. That will give us enough time to do some digging, literally."

"That's a crazy idea, Cedric."

"Are you coming or not?"

"Yes, but only to stop you from breaking into the house and lifting up the floorboards when you discover the flowerbeds empty."

SCENE 3

ELIZABETH'S GARDEN

"We'll need this." said Cedric emerging from the rear of the shed carrying a spade.

"What for?"

"How else can I dig up the flowerbeds, Penelope?"

"You're not seriously going to dig up her flowerbeds? Look at all those lovely marigolds and begonias. What will Lizzie think?"

"We'll blame it on moles. I'll start with the one with the snapdragons, I've never really liked them."

As he picked up the spade ready to plunge it into the flowerbed they heard a loud crashing sound.

"What was that?" squealed Penelope.

"It came from the side of the house."

"Are they back already?"

"We'd better hide."

"HELP!"

"That sounds like Robert."

They ran across the grass to the side of the house and saw a ladder lying on the ground.

"UP HERE!"

Robert was hanging from an upper windowsill by his fingertips.

"Quick. Cedric, get the ladder up," said Penelope.

Cedric picked up the ladder and elevated it until it was within Robert's reach. He cautiously put his foot onto one of the rungs.

"Keep a hold of the bottom, Cedric," urged Penelope.

Robert clambered onto the ladder and descended.

"Are you alright, Robert?" asked Penelope concerned.

"I'm ok, just a bit shaken."

"What happened? asked Cedric inspecting the rungs of the ladder.

"I don't know, the ladder just fell away."

"Were you overreaching?"

"No, I didn't think I was."

"Another lucky escape, Robert," said Penelope.

"Well, they say bad luck always runs in threes."

"Hopefully," muttered Cedric.

"What were you doing up there anyway?" asked Penelope.

"Fixing the roof tiles, like Elizabeth wanted."

"I thought you were going to Lady Thorndyke's today?"

"No, Elizabeth got the date wrong, it's tomorrow."

"So .Lizzie is here?" said Cedric suspiciously.

"No, she went riding."

"See," said Penelope glaring at Cedric.

"It's lucky you were here. I don't know how much longer I could have held on to the windowsill for."

"I suppose so," murmured Cedric.

"Penelope! Cedric! What are you doing here?" said Elixabeth suddenly appearing through the side door just below the ladder.

"Umm," stumbled Cedric.

"We came to visit you Lizzie," said Penelope hurriedly.

"You visited yesterday. Why have you come again today?"

"Umm."

"This is a surprise visit," continued Penelope.

"Why?"

"Umm"

"It's just as well we did, Robert was hanging from the window ledge," said Penelope quickly changing the topic.

"Hanging from the window ledge?"

"Yes, the ladder had fallen."

"Oh, Robert, you are clumsy."

"I don't know how it happened. I thought you had gone riding," said Robert.

"I came back early because Bonnie was playing up, she's a very temperamental horse."

"So, you must have been here when the ladder fell," said Cedric suspiciously.

"What are you doing with that spade, Cedric?"

"Umm, I was going to borrow it."

"For what?"

"Digging."

"Where?"

"My garden."

"You have decking all over your garden."

"I was thinking of changing it back to grass."

"I thought you hate grass, that's why you had decking laid?"

"Umm."

"Elizabeth, I think I'd better get back inside and get a calming cup of tea," said Robert shakily.

"Of course, dear," she said escorting Robert back inside.

"We'll go, Lizzie, let you look after Robert," said Penelope. "See you another time."

"Just put the spade back when you have finished with it, Cedric."

"Ok, maybe you're right about my garden, Lizzie. I'll put it back and leave the decking for now," called Cedric as she disappeared.

"Perhaps you can use it to dig yourself into a bigger hole," quipped Penelope. "Just put the spade back and let's get out of here. You need to stop this suspicious nonsense."

Cedric walked across the garden and disappeared around the shed.

"Do you want some berries," he said returning with a handful of small black coloured berries.

"Where did you get those?"

"They were on a plant growing behind the shed," he replied lifting one to his mouth.

"Don't eat them" said Penelope quickly.. "They're belladonna berries, deadly nightshade."

Cedric stared anxiously at the house.

ACT III

SCENE 1

BACK AT CEDRIC AND PENELOPE'S HOUSE

"That's how she's doing it, Penelope. She poisons them with deadly nightshade and buries them under the flowerbeds."

"Don't be silly, Cedric."

"Those flowerbeds appeared at the exact same time that her previous husbands vanished."

"Can you really see Lizzie digging a hole big enough for a body?"

"She must get them to dig the holes themselves."

"What! And then I suppose they considerately clamber into the hole and whack themselves on the head with the spade."

"No, I told you, she poisons them with the berries, probably in the house."

"How does she get the bodies to the hole?"

"Umm, puts them in the wheelbarrow. Even Lizzie could manage that. Yes, she wheels them out to the hole in the dead of night and tips them in. Then puts the soil on top and plants some bulbs."

"Probably hasn't even got a wheelbarrow."

"Yes, there is, I saw it at the back of the shed."

"Sounds like a lot of dirty work, I can't imagine Lizzie doing any of it, Cedric."

"Then how do you explain the deadly nightshade growing behind the shed."

"I've never known Lizzie go anywhere near the shed let alone behind it."

"I bet she took Charlie Fletcher's boots to the quarry once he was in the hole and detonated the explosion herself. And I expect she set Tommy Tibbs's boat adrift as soon as he was safely underground."

"How does she get them to eat the poison berries?"

"Umm, a fruit salad?"

"Hmmm."

"No, I know, she poisons the wine, just like Macbeth did to the invading Danes."

"It all seems a bit far-fetched to me, Cedric."

"How do you explain the ladder falling?"

"Something wrong with it, maybe a broken rung?"

"I inspected it myself, it was fine, Penelope."

"Robert overbalanced?"

"More likely is that Lizzie came out through the side door and pushed it. She could have easily disappeared back inside once the deed was done. She didn't come to his aid when he called for help and she must have been closer than us."

"She might have only just returned from the stables."

"I doubt she even went to the stables."

"What are we going to do then?"

"Go back there."

"We can't, we struggled to explain our presence this afternoon."

"We'll go at night."

"When?"

"Tonight."

SCENE 2

BACK IN ELIZABETH'S GARDEN

THE DEAD OF NIGHT

"Cedric, I can't see a thing. Turn the torch on."

"Not yet, Penelope, they might see it."

"It's 3am, the house is in complete darkness. They have clearly gone to bed."

"Nevertheless, let's wait until we are behind the shed, just in case."

"Quite exciting really, now I know how it feels to be a cat burglar," whispered Penelope as they crept around the back of the shed.

"OWW."

"Are you ok, Cedric?"

"Banged my knee on the wheelbarrow," he replied grimacing and furiously rubbing his leg.

"Turn the torch on for goodness sake, we're out of view of the house now."

"Ok,"

"Where's the deadly nightshade?" asked Penelope following the beam all around.

"It's here somewhere, let me think where I saw it. Ah, there it is," said Cedric illuminating the plant.

"Where are the berries?"

"There were about twenty of them, they are all gone."

"Oh, Cedric, do you think we are too late?"

"Quick, check the wheelbarrow for any evidence," he said shining the light onto it.

"Like what?"

"I don't know, torn clothing, bits of hair, blood spots."

"All I can see is encrusted dirt and clumps of mud."

"Ok, forget the wheelbarrow, let's see if there is a fresh flowerbed."

"What about the torch light?"

"We'll have to take the chance, we are talking about murder, Penelope."

He scanned the garden until the beam lit up a freshly dug flowerbed.

SCENE 3

LADY THORNDYKE'S HOUSE

AFTER THE FUNERAL

"Just three weeks ago I was the best man at the wedding and now I'm at the funeral," exclaimed Jack knocking back a whisky.

"It's dreadful," said Penelope.

"I remember when we were boys we were hiking with the scouts and Robert had eaten a belladonna berry from a plant that was growing wild. He only had one before the scout leader stopped him but it made him quite sick. You'd think he would have known. Well, that's the end of his money troubles."

"He had money problems?" asked Cedric surprised.

"Almost bankrupt. He told me after he got back from his honeymoon, asked me for money, didn't want Elizabeth to know. He had lost a lot of clients as more and more office workers started working from home. Empty offices meant he had no-one to sell the sandwiches to. Meeting Elizabeth was a stroke of luck. Do you know the last thing he did for her was to dig a flowerbed? What a terrible accident. Anyway, I'm going to get another drink."

"There's no way it was an accident," said Cedric as Jack moved away. "But we'll never be able to prove now how the poison was administered, Penelope."

"The coroner's verdict was death by misadventure, didn't know what the berries were and ate them."

"You just heard what Jack said, he had a bad experience with deadly nightshade already. Clearly he would have known what the berries were and their effect. The motive was clearly money. Let's have a toast in memory."

They raised their glasses in tribute.

"TO LIZZIE!"

VALENTINE'S

TALE

I'm going to do it, I'm going to ask her out. She can only say no. Probably will say no. Well, ok, her choice, she doesn't have to go out with me. But there's no reason she will say "no," I'm a perfectly nice guy, I've got a good job, my own house and I'm reasonable looking for 33. A lot of men my age are going grey or balding. Just look at my thick mop of hair and full beard, ok it's a bit bushier than most but beards are all the rage these days, and not a grey fleck in sight. And because it is thick it's lovely and soft, not rough and bristly like many. Kissing men with rough beards must be like having your lips pressed against sandpaper. I'm sure Jennifer would enjoy kissing me, I would certainly enjoy kissing her. Why shouldn't it happen? Ok, I might be a bit on the short side. That's it, she will say no, bound to say I'm too short. For a while I wore block heeled platform boots but kept getting asked if I was a roadie for the Bay City Rollers. The cheek of it, I'm 33 not 73. Anyway, I'm waiting for her outside her office building. No, I'm not stalking her, I work in the office across the road and was just dropping off some documents before I go home. Besides I've known her since we were at school. She always seemed to have a boyfriend but I know from a contact in her office that she is single at present.

Here she comes now, just look at her flowing blonde hair, she is so elegant in her matching navy skirt and jacket with a stylish black handbag hanging from her shoulder and her long shapely legs going into black stiletto shoes. Her angelic face radiates with beauty, Helen of Troy reincarnated. Despite the stack of folders in her arms she glides gracefully across the marble floor. I can smell her intoxicating perfume as she draws near.

"Jennifer, hi."

"Oh. Hi, Alan."

"Let me carry your folders for you."

"Sure."

"This is just like school when I used to carry your books home, do you remember?"

"I remember, my car is at the end of the street."

"What are all these folders, are you taking work home?"

"God, no. I said I would drop them off at the lawyer's office."

"Is it on your way home?"

"Not particularly. There is a promotion coming up and I want to look good."

That's another great thing about Jennifer, she is so keen to get on in life. She worked late with her boss every Friday night for three months to get her last promotion, even going to his house when his wife was away, such dedication.

"Actually, the office is out of the way, and the rush hour traffic will be terrible. I wonder if maybe you could…no, it's too much to ask."

Look at those beautiful sparkling eyes and long fluttering eyelashes.

"I could deliver them for you?"

"Alan, you're the best. Well, this is my car here."

I watch as she quickly opens the door and gets in. It's now or never, she might have another boyfriend by tomorrow. She closes the door and starts the engine. I lower my head to the window struggling not to drop the fodders.

"Jennifer."

The window winds down.

"What is it Alan? " she replies glancing at her slim gold watch.

"Um, well, I was wondering, if maybe, if you're free."

"Hurry up, Alan, I want to get home before *Real Housewives* starts."

"Um, well, if you would like to go out with me."

"Where?"

"Um, maybe the cinema or a restaurant."

"What, like a date?"

"Well, yes, kind of."

"You're a nice guy Alan, but I have a policy of not going out with guys with beards."

I watch as her car speeds away.

Five minutes later I'm sitting in a long tail-back of traffic, the folders piled on the passenger seat. I knew she would say no, it's this beard, what girl wants a man with a big bushy beard. Possibly a woman heavily into lumberjacks but certainly not a goddess like Jennifer.

I finally ger home with my stomach rumbling after two hours of being stuck in traffic. A quick bite to eat before I pass out on the floor and I'm stood in the bathroom looking into the mirror with razor in hand. My beard has taken years of careful cultivation, still it will all be worth it to go out with Jennifer.

Here I am back outside Jennifer's office block. I can't wait for her to see my clean shaven face, although in truth the cold February air is chilling my newly exposed skin, I hope she comes soon before my cheeks go numb. There she is, the living embodiment of Venus, gliding across the foyer in her light grey suit, a burgundy bag over her shoulder and the lights making her golden rings sparkle. It's amazing how many rings she has on her hands, I think there might be two on one finger.

"Jennifer!"

"Alan, oh my God, I hardly recognised you without your beard."

"Do you like it?" I say enthusiastically.

"Well, it's different."

"I did it for you."

"What?"

"You said you would go out with me if I shaved my beard," I say beaming expectantly.

"I didn't exactly say that."

"We could go out for a meal."

"I don't know."

"That restaurant in Main Street, The Orchard."

"The one with the Michelin Star owned by that celebrity chef?"

"I've heard it's very good."

"And very exclusive, I don't think you will get a table in there, Alan."

"I do their accounts, they have often invited me but I have never had anyone to go with."

"Well, ok, if you can get a table, I'd love to go."

"I'll ring them right now."

Jennifer waits while I get out my mobile phone and call. I hope I can get a reservation..

"They can give us a table tomorrow evening at eight."

"Great."

Jennifer looks even more beautiful with her radiant smile and sparkling eyes, she must be as happy as me that we are finally going on a date together.

"I'll pick you up at half past seven."

"It's only a short drive, make it a quarter to eight."

"A quarter to eight it is."

I pull up in front of a small, detached house, Jennifer moved back in with her parents after her last break up. I get out and see Jennifer coming down the driveway, the outside light illuminating her cherubic face and her long blonde hair cascading around her shoulders. Her ruby lips shine and her black mascara highlights her twinkling eyes. As she walks gracefully in her stiletto heels her black dress shimmers under a gentle breeze. I hold the door open for her.

"Quarter to eight exactly," I say looking at my watch.

"Always punctual, Alan."

"I never like to be late anywhere."

!I'm really looking forward to this, I've never been to a Michelin Star restaurant before. I wonder if we'll see any celebrities."

"I'm just glad you're here with me."

"Maybe a pop star or a famous footballer."

"You look very nice."

"Or someone off a reality TV show."

At the restaurant we are seated in the corner.

"So, you're back living with your mum and dad," I say.

"Oh; yea," she replies craning her neck about the room. "Do you think that's the guy off *Love Island*?"

"Umm, I don't know, I don't really watch reality TV. I expect they are glad to have you back?"

"I suppose so," says Jennifer getting out her phone and taking a photo of the guy who may or may not in fact be on Love Island.

The waiter brings the menu.

"Look at all these exotic dishes," gushes Jennifer. "Wagyu Fillet Steak, White Truffles, Lobster and Sevruga Caviar."

I'm more interested in the exotic prices and wondering if I will have to sell my car to pay the bill. Still, it's all for Jenifer I remind myself.

The food was very good I have to admit.

"Where are you living now, Alan?"

"Cedar Avenue."

"Those new luxury apartments," gasps Jennifer opening her eyes wide. "They are expensive, how much is your rent?"

"I don't pay rent, it's mine."

"You must be earning loads of money, Alan."

"Not loads, but I saved hard for a deposit, and spend very little. I always buy the supermarkets own brands of food and don't go out very much, just once a week with Jerry to the pub."

"I'd love to see it."

These words are magic to my ears, Jennifer wants to visit me.

"Great, we can arrange a date, maybe on the weekend."

"I was thinking now."

I can hardly believe it, fantastic.

Unbelievable, Jennifer Grey is in my apartment. I notice her screwing up her face as she looks around the sparsely furnished sitting room. She sits down in one of the old second hand armchairs I got on eBay.

" I could not afford much furniture when I moved in," I mumble, slightly embarrassed.

"You could do with a sofa, maybe a nice, big corner one."

"I've been meaning to buy some new stuff but it's all so expensive and I don't get many visitors, in fact, it's only really Jerry."

"It's a big room you just need some decor, maybe a coffee table and some lamps. Let's go on to the balcony."

"It's a bit cold."

"You'll be fine," she says getting up and opening the glass doors.

"What a wonderful view!" she enthuses, gazing out over the river.

"It's one of the reasons I bought it, it's so quiet and tranquil here,"

I glance at my watch.

"Anyway, I had better drive you back to your parents."

"I could stay here," she coos, looking at me with fluttering eyelashes.

"I only have one bedroom."

"That's all we'll need."

Amazing. Sat at my desk the following morning all I can think about is that Jennifer Grey was in my bed last night. Not just in my bed but naked in my bed. I look around the office, I am sure my face has gone red. Even better, she wants to move in. It's like a dream, me, Alan Scudder, living with Jennifer Grey. I have already given her my spare key and have a photo of her on my desk wearing a little black cocktail dress. It's hard concentrating on my work today, as I admire her photo, I cannot get home fast enough. Unfortunately, my boss is off with stress so I have to work late, I wonder if Jennifer will be there when I get back.

As I drive up I can see the light in the sitting room window, incredible. I park and race up the stairs. Outside the front door I can hear Jennifer's voice coming from inside

"It's ok here, though the furniture is ghastly."

I insert my key and enter the apartment. Jennifer is standing in front of the balcony window talking on her mobile phone. The light shines radiantly off her blonde locks.

"I'll talk to you later."

"Sorry, I had to work late, Peter, my boss, is off with stress again."

"You will need to get some new furniture now I'm staying here. I can't be expected to sit in those tatty old things," she says looking disgustedly at the armchairs.

"I suppose so."

"We can go shopping tomorrow."

"Umm, I have to work tomorrow."

"On a Saturday!"

"Like I said,, Peter is off sick."

"Who's Peter?"

"My boss."

Was she listening at all to what I said?

"Fine. Give me your credit card."

Her hand is held stiffly out. I suppose I could do with some new furniture, although in truth I was happy with what I had, I guess things are different now."

I reach into my wallet and give her my credit card.

"Now, what's for dinner?" she asks eagerly.

"Umm I normally just microwave something out of the freezer."

"No, that's no good. We'll have to go out, I'll get my coat."

What a tiring day, I can't say I enjoy working Saturdays very much. At least I'm coming back to Jennifer, I'm the luckiest man in the world.

I look around the sitting room in stunned silence. Jennifer is spread out on a blue velvet corner sofa. My first thought is it looks expensive. In front of her, on a new mahogany table, stands an open bottle of wine and a long stemmed crystal glass which looks new too.

"Get a glass and we can celebrate our new look," she says raising the glass and holding it aloft by way of a toast.

"I'm not sure blue goes with the room," I say cautiously.

"Teal."

"Pardon?"

"It's teal, not blue."

Looks blue to me.

"How did you get it delivered so quickly?" I ask.

"I paid extra for immediate delivery."

More bloody expense.

"Don't worry I made some money."

"How?" I ask nervously.

"I sold the armchairs for £50."

"I paid £100 for them."

"You were robbed."

I certainly have been.

"Anyway you will be earning money now with your new job," she continues.

"What new job?"

"Your boss's."

"He's not officially gone yet."

"You said he was getting fired."

"I don't think I said that, although they are pretty ruthless."

"Your firm have obviously already decided, why else would you be in doing his job today."

"That's just temporary, besides I don't know if I would want to do it permanently."

"Why not?"

"It's longer hours and quite stressful."

"Don't you want us to have nice things?"

"Well, yes, I suppose so."

"Well, then it's settled."

"Even if he goes there is no guarantee I would be offered the job."

"I'm sure you will, you need to be more ambitious, Alan. You need to look the part, we can start by getting you some new clothes."

Jennifer looks me up and down from my clumpy brown brogues to my white polyester shirt.

"We can go shopping tomorrow. Then all you need to do is keep doing the overtime and they are sure to give you the job."

In truth I'm quite content doing what I'm doing and not having a teal corner sofa, but I suppose Jennifer knows best.

Well, this is different. I'm stood in the shop in a navy blue Armani suit looking at my reflection in the full-length mirror.

"Oh, yes, very sharp," coos Jennifer as I discretely peek at the price label.

"I don't know," I say trying not to pass out on the floor.

"You have no style, Alan. It's perfect, we'll take it. You can wear it tonight when we go out."

"Tonight? It's Sunday, I always go to the pub with Jerry on a Sunday."

"This is our first weekend together and you spend Saturday working and now you want to spend Sunday in the pub?" she said raising her voice.

I'm conscious of other shoppers and staff looking at us.

"Fine, I'll ring him and tell I can't make it tonight," I say quietly.

"That's better, now let's look for a nice bag for me, I saw a very chic Gucci one in the window."

Well, that was fast, after only a week I have been given the boss's job permanently after Peter was fired as expected. I think the new clothes helped and the photo of Jennifer. The senior partner kept staring at it while he was offering me the job. It will mean more work for me but Jennifer will be pleased. The job also comes with a new office with a view overlooking the city and a luxurious cream leather chair. I recline back and survey the spacious room with the large oak desk and Yucca plant in the corner. I will be dealing with our richer clients now I have been promoted, in fact this morning I am meeting with Neville Montgomery, not even fifty and already a multi-millionaire.

There is a knock on my door and it opens.

"Mr. Montgomery to see you."

"Thank you, Tim. Alan Scudder, very pleased to meet you Mr. Montgomery," I say getting up and extending my hand warmly.

As he takes it I am struck by the firmness of his grip and the gold Rolex on his wrist. His fingers are perfectly manicured, his black hair slicked back and his beard meticulously trimmed around his jawline.

"Neville is fine," he says in a voice that is both calm and assertive. "So, you have replaced Peter."

"Yes, that's right."

"And inherited his office and spectacular view."

He walks behind the desk and looks out through the window.

"Can I get you something to drink?"

"No, thank you. I just wanted to see who was dealing with my account now."

He turns and looks at the desk, picking up the picture of Jennifer. His eyes widen as he casts his eye from the picture to me and back to the picture.

"Your wife?"

"My girlfriend, Jennifer," I say proudly.

"Jennifer," he muses putting the picture back on the desk before glancing at his watch and moving to the door.

"Well, again, it was very nice to meet you."

He stops and turns.

"I'm having a few people over to my house Friday evening, why don't you come. We can talk more then."

"I'd be delighted."

"Oh and bring your girlfriend."

Friday night and we are driving to the party. I have only been doing my new job for a week and already I'm exhausted, I don't want to be here too late as I have to go in to the office again tomorrow, I've aged about ten years judging by the deepening bags under my eyes. In stark contrast Jennifer looks striking in a new red dress she bought straight after I told her about the invitation, lucky I got a pay rise with my new job.

"It's money well spent," says Jennifer applying some more red lipstick. "We wouldn't have got an invitation if it wasn't for me. You're going up in the world now, I don't think you can be spending your time in the local pub with the likes of Jerry Webb."

"I've known Jerry a long time," I reply stifling a yawn.

"I remember him from school with his greasy hair and dirty clothes. What does he do now?"

"He's a mechanic."

We turn into the gravel driveway that leads up to Neville Montgomery's house, although mansion would be a more accurate description. Arched Georgian windows stretch along three storeys of the façade.

"Can you honestly see Jerry Webb in a place like this, unless he was here to fix the cars?"

I detect a hint of sarcasm but let it slide.

It's true it's not really Jerry's kind of thing, not sure it's mine either.

"Alan, glad you could make it," says Neville Montgomery shaking me by the hand.

"This is my girlfriend, Jennifer."

"Very pleased to meet you," he says shaking her hand and holding it longer than necessary in my opinion. "Come and get a drink."

The room is very opulent with a Persian rug on the floor and gold framed paintings on the walls. There is even a grand piano on a slightly raised level. There are a lot of men in dinner suits and woman in ball gowns. I get talking to, or more accurately, talked at, by s merchant banker who informs me that he is at the number one ranked investment institution and that he doubled his bonus this year, only increasing my desire to yawn. I can see Jennifer talking and laughing with Neville Montgomery by the piano. With seemingly little persuasion he sits down and starts to play a classical piece. I find a comfy armchair to plonk down in.

"What a wonderful house!" coos Jennifer as we drive home. "And what a magnificent host, did you hear him playing Moonlight Sonata? Just beautiful."

"Mmmm," I mumble barely able to keep my eyes open now.

"And best of all he has invited us to go on his yacht tomorrow."

"I have to work tomorrow."

"Ok, I'll go by myself then."

This a new turn of events. Still he has a beard and that's a no-no for Jennifer.

****

Over the next few weeks my work load gets heavier and heavier resulting in more and more time in the office. I drive home after yet another Saturday slaving away. This job is killing me, the long hours, the weekend work, I haven't seen Jerry for over a month.

Jennifer seems to be spending more time in the company of Neville Montgomery. I open the door to the apartment.

"Jennifer!"

No reply, probably out with bloody Neville Montgomery again.

I go into the bedroom to hang my jacket up. The wardrobe is half empty, all Jennifer's clothes have gone, no dresses on hangers, no shoes on the racks. I look around the room, everything of hers has gone. Panicked I rush into the lounge, propped up on the coffee table is a note.

> *This is not really working out Alan.*
> *You are never around anymore, always*
> *working and when you do get back you*
> *are always too tired to do anything.*

Hurriedly, I get my phone.

"Jennifer, we can work this out," I blurt.

"No, Alan, we've outgrown each other, you have your career now."

"I only took this job because you told me to, I was quite happy in my old job. I even shaved my beard off for you."

"I'm sorry, Alan, I've decided to go away with Neville."

"But he has a beard."

"Not for long."

REFLECTIONS FROM A BRIDGE

NATURE DOES, WITHOUT PURPOSE,

WITHOUT MEANING

EVERYTHING IS NATURE

The tramp trudged slowly along the side of the railway track feeling the cold, night air chill his aging body. He pulled the torn overcoat tighter as his breath mixed with the surrounding mist so it was impossible to distinguish which was which. On and on he roamed in this desolate place made even more so in the stillness and darkness. The only sound was that of his worn boots as the gravel crunched below with each step. Up ahead he saw the bridge high above the track, a sight he had not seen in many years. He gazed at the lamps spaced out behind the metal railing shrouded with mist giving a shimmering glow. Below the hazy light he saw a man pacing back and forth. He stopped walking and watched the man meandering up and down, occasionally pausing and leaning over the railing, staring at the track far below, then burying his face in his hands, before pacing back and forth once more. The tramp continued walking, drawing ever nearer. At the foot of the bridge he climbed the metal ladder that was affixed to the brickwork. The ladder was rusted, creaking and vibrating with each step that he took. The icy rungs freezing his bare hands as he ascended. Finally he emerged on the westside of the bridge. The mist had thickened and he could only just about see the indistinct outline of the man slumped over the railings. The tramp shuffled slowly towards him. As he got closer he could see that the man was wearing a crumpled, dark grey, business suit, his shirt collar was undone and his tie hung loosely from his neck. His black brogues were elegant but splattered with mud. His face was young but unshaven, in fact, he struck the tramp as being just as dishevelled as he was. He stood beside him and just looked at him slumped over the railing with his face resting on his hands and staring blankly at the tracks far below.

"I have thought about it many times."

The man stayed silent and motionless, he did not look at him.

"Not recently, but many years ago," continued the tramp.

"Why didn't you?" said the man coldly still looking down over the railings.

"It wasn't my path."

The man turned his head slowly to the side and observed the tramp. He could see his tatty coat with a tear down one sleeve and buttons missing from the front. His trousers were dirty and creased and his boots were shabby and worn down at the heels. His face was old and wrinkled, etched with deep lines and his uneven, dark beard flecked with grey and white. Below his hat with the brim broken down on one side hung long strands of greying hair down to his shoulders.

"And this is your path, to be a tramp?"

"Yes."

"I would have chosen a different path."

"I did not choose the path, no-one chooses their path."

"That's nonsense."

"Tell me, did you want to be here tonight?"

The man fell silent his face becoming more desolate. His head turned back to the track.

"No," he murmured.

"It was your path that brought you here tonight."

"Financial ruin brought me here tonight. I worked so hard accumulating money, my entire life."

"You were living your life wrong, like many people, worshipping the false God of money."

"We all need money."

"In the artificial society we have created money is useful in avoiding starving or freezing to death. However, the importance of money has been elevated to an exulted and undeserved status. In the 200,00 year existence of man money has only been around for about 6.000 and he survived. Even more recently, 600 years ago do you think the native tribes of America had need of money living in their communities, building their own shelter, sourcing their own food, making their own clothes?"

"That was different, now you need money and to work hard to get it."

"Tell me did you play the board game Monopoly as a child?"

"Yes, I often won."

"Did you ever just move around the board and not buy property, not build houses and hotels, not acquire money?"

"The point of the game is to buy property and build houses and hotels and acquire money."

"You played Monopoly as a child and you are still playing it, the hat became your role model. You are living your life in the pursuit of a thing that is artificial. Money only exists in your mind, or rather, our collective minds. Money has no value except in the mind. Value has no meaning except in our minds. A diamond exists in nature and has existed for millions of years. We can dig it up, polish and cut it and might delight in the way in sparkles but its monetary value is artificial in the collective agreement of our minds. Because of your belief in it and now its loss your path has brought you here tonight."

"Circumstances outside of my control led me here tonight," said the man sombrely.

"Ah, control, the illusion of man."

"I used to be in control, I had money, a good job, a nice house, a beautiful wife...I lost them all."

His words quietened and trailed away to nothingness.

"What do we really control? You are not even in control of your own body. You do not control your liver function, kidney function, your hair and nails growing. You do not decide that your heart should beat or lungs breathe. You do not control the blood flowing or clotting when the skin is cut."

"Maybe not, but I should have been able to control my life."

"It was your path to lose them, your perceived control is nothing more than a deception."

"That's rubbish."

"Nature controls you, not the other way around. If you could control nature, you would be God."

"I just made wrong choices, that is all. If I could turn the clock back I would do things differently, make different choices, better choices."

"No, you would do exactly the same things and make exactly the same choices."

"No, I would make completely different ones."

"Let's see. Suppose you conduct an experiment and you get a result. Now suppose you conduct the experiment again with all the factors being exactly the same, what would be the result?"

The man paused and thought.

"The same result, I guess."

"Exactly."

"But I am different now, I would be the different factor, therefore the result would be different, better."

"That would not be turning back the clock, that would be going back in time as the person you are now, not as the person you were then. What you are really wish is that you were a different person then, because, of course, a different person would make different decisions. The person you were would do the same things, you always do whatever you think is best from the position you are in at any given moment. No-one acts against what they believe to be in their best interest, But you never know what is in your best interest. But the truth is there are no decisions only the path.

"So; are you saying I was destined to come to this bridge tonight?"

"No, not destined. To say it is your destiny is to presuppose that it is preordained. Designed or created. That would imply there is a creator or designer, There is none, it is your path and could not be any different."

"Are you saying I did not decide to come here tonight?"

"Yes."

"So, what decided?"

"Nothing decided. Nature brought you here tonight."

"For what reason."

"No reason. Nature does, without purpose, without meaning. Nature does not decide, it has no plan. To say there is a plan is to imply there is an end, a point. There is none. Nature has no end, no goal, it just does, without purpose."

"What do you mean by nature?"

"Everything is nature. Everything in the universe: the stars, the suns, the elements. They are all without purpose. What is the purpose of a tree, what is the purpose of a cloud, what is the purpose of the sun?"

"The sun heats and lights the planet, without the sun we would not exist."

"That is the typical human centric view of man, everything exists for the benefit of man even if it is merely to be discovered by man, like a quest or a puzzle to be solved. From this human centric view you have stated what the sun does but it is not its purpose, it has no purpose, it just exists as a part of nature."

"It is God that made these things."

"You can use whatever word you want, God, nature, the universe. But it is everything. I prefer the word nature. People are too apt to think in religious terms when they use the word God. Crediting God with being the creator and therefore the universe as a creation with purpose and meaning. That is why the word God is unhelpful in understanding. Nature does not create, it just does, without purpose, without meaning. Everything is nature."

"I don't believe it."

"Is it so hard? Man thinks of himself as being separate from nature. He thinks of nature as being over there, that forest, that stream. Certainly not the city, the buildings, the roads, they are not nature, he believes. But this is wrong. The bricks for the houses and the tar for the roads come from and are still a part of nature. Parts of nature reformed and reconstituted. Just like a tree can be metamorphosed into chairs, tables, paper.

Man is not connected to the ground like a tree or a flower. He is not part of the ground like a mountain or a valley. Nonetheless, he is a part of nature. Everything is connected, Man is surrounded by air like a fish is surrounded by water. And just like water goes inside the fish so air goes inside of man. Air is both inside and outside of us. Imagine if man could see the air, he would realise that he is exactly like the fish in water. Even if man jumped in the air there would still be air connecting him to the ground."

"If nature is everything, and does everything, then you are saying there is no free will."

"Is it so strange? From where do our ideas come? Do we really control them? We can see that we do not control our internal organs, our hair and nails growing. We must consider that similarly we do not control our thoughts. We are merely conscious of them, watching our lives play out as though we were watching ourselves in a film on a screen. And just like a film if we were to rewind the reel and watch the film again it would be exactly the same. So, our life would be exactly the same. A film does not change, no matter how many times you play it. So, it is with our lives. How could it be different? Remember the scientific principle, if all the factors stay the same the result will always be the same.

We are not responsible for our perceived successes or failures, for we do not control them. I say perceived because what even constitutes success and failure is unclear. A man gets a high paying job in a plush office block and is then killed when the building catches fire. Is that success or failure? You can call it what you want but he had no control. He did not appoint himself to the job, he did not cause the fire.

Everything that happens, happens by chance. You met your wife because, by chance, you happened to be in a certain place at a certain time. You could just have easily been in a different place at that time. Or in that place but at a different time so your paths never ever crossed.

Some people will call this fate, but it is not, it is the path. Fate suggests there is a grand plan, a design for the universe, there is not.

Think of all the infinite possibilities of the place you could be at any given time. You think there are an infinite number of possibilities, but there is only one, the path, the one that is, the others do not exist, never existed and never will exist. To think back on what might have been is futile. It is to think that there were and are other paths, there are not.

Even if you could go on another path, like the man killed in the fire you could not know and cannot know, if that path is better or worse.

In fact, there is no better or worse, there are merely parts of the path where perceived worse parts are links to perceived better parts. Man dies and that is not the end of the path. Everything is nature and the body is metamorphosed like water is changed into steam by boiling, the water is still part of nature in a different form, and man is still part of nature in a different form. Parts of the body eaten by the worms become part of the worms. The worms then eaten by the birds become part of the birds and so on. And not just to become parts of worms and birds but part of everything. It is a never ending cycle. The parts that constituted your body become part of the soil, the trees the grass, the air. A single entity that is nature, with no beginning and no end. Ther hair on your head is not the same hair as a year ago, nor the nails of your fingers and toes, nor your skin. Yet they all still exist as part of nature transformed into something else. So, we can say nothing ever really dies, meaning a thing cannot become nothing.

The path led you here tonight and the path will take you on from here tonight in one form or another."

The man continued leaning over the railings, silently looking at the tracks far below. In the distance could be heard the train speeding through the darkness. The tramp listened as the sound of the wheels on the track grew louder. Without speaking he moved away from the railings and walked slowly from the bridge. As the train roared below the bridge he disappeared into the mist, he never looked back.

CEDRIC AND THE VAMPIRES

Characters

Cedric, thirtysomething socialite

Penelope, Cedric's wife

Darius, new neighbour

Adelina, wife of Darius

Daphne, friend of Cedric & Penelope

Sebastian, Daphne's husband

ACT I

SCENE 1

CEDRIC AND PENELOPE'S HOUSE

Cedric is peeking from behind the curtains at the house opposite.

"I'm telling you, Penelope, they're vampires."

"They are not vampires, Cedric, you are always imagining things."

"They must have moved in while we were away last week."

"See, you have not even met them."

"That's because they don't go out in the day."

"Stop spying on them and move away from the window."

"Look, all their curtains are closed and it's the middle of the afternoon. Probably asleep in their coffins."

"Maybe they work nightshifts."

"Yes, prowling the streets looking for victims."

"I saw them at the start of the week, they seemed normal to me."

"When was that, you didn't tell me?"

"I don't know, Monday or Tuesday evening."

"I bet that was after sunset."

"Well, yes, it would be, it's dark by six o'clock, be even earlier next week. That reminds me, we must remember to put the clocks back one hour tonight."

"I bet you haven't seen them since."

"Well, no."

"That's because they're vampires, only come out after dark. Look at the size of the boot on their car! How many bodies do you think would fit in that?"

"Come away from the window, Cedric."

"Alright, but I'm going to watch them tonight when they come out to feast."

"We are going to dinner at Daphne's this evening."

"Daphy's?"

"I told you yesterday, you were probably too busy spying on the neighbours to listen."

" I don't spy."

"What are you doing right now then, peeking from behind the curtains?"

"Neighbourhood watch."

"Neighbourhood watch?"

"Yes, ensuring no vampires are in the area."

"Come away from the window, Cedric, before you get accused of being a peeping Tom, again."

"That was a complete overreaction by Mrs. Fotheringham, as if I would have any interest ogling a seventy year old woman."

"That policeman who came took a different view."

"Anyway she's away in her holiday home in France for the next three months. Probably just as well, she would be easy prey for the vampires."

"Hmm."

"Who else is going to Daphy's bash tonight?"

"Just us."

"That means I have to endure that oik of a husband."

"Better not refer to Sebastian as an oik."

"He's such a show off, I don't know what she sees in him."

"He is very successful, Cedric."

"He's a philistine, always bragging about how much things cost him. He knows the price of everything and the value of nothing."

"Well, he is very rich, Cedric."

"And he lets everyone know it. Hopefully the vampires will get him first."

SCENE 2

DAPHNE AND SEBASTIAN'S HOUSE

"What do you think of my new watch, Cedric?"

"Very nice, Sebastian," said Cedric unenthusiastically.

"A real Rolex, handcrafted in 18 karat yellow gold. How much do you think it cost?"

"I really don't know."

"Go on, guess."

"£10,000."

"Higher."

"£20,000," said Cedric wondering what was the least amount of time it was acceptable to stay for.

"£30,000! More than your car."

"I drive a BMW."

"Yes, but it's getting on a bit, do you still have to crank a handle to get it started?"

"Sebastian dear, open a bottle of champagne and I'll put on some music. Mozart alright, Penelope?"

"Lovely, Daphne."

Sebastian and Daphne go to the other side of the room.

"I've only just stepped over the threshold and he's already shoving his watch in my face," whispered Cedric to Penelope.

"Be nice."

"Try this," said Sebastian returning and ceremoniously presenting a silver platter with four crystal flutes sparkling with champagne. "A 1985 Bollinger, I think you will find this to be a very good year."

"That's quite exquisite, Sebastain," said Penelope. "A subtle hint of pear and oak."

"And apple."

"Oh, yes," said Penelope taking another sip. "A light trace of apple too."

"Let's sit at the table and I'll tell Charles to serve dinner," said Daphne.

"We ordered a case of these from Harrods," said Sebastain placing the bottle in the middle of the table as they all took their places at each side, Cedric opposite Penelope and Daphne opposite Sebastian. "What do you think, Cedric?"

"Very good," replied Cedric who really thought it tasted a bit like Lambrusco.

"Made entirely from Pinot Noir grapes that are maintained by hand. £2,000 a bottle."

Cedric sighed and looked around the room only surprised there was not a price tag on each piece of furniture.

(Later in the evening)

"That was a wonderful dinner, Daphne, my compliments to the chef," praised Penelope. "We have not had lobster for a while. What was the name of that delicious sauce again?"

"Beurre blanc sauce."

"Oh yes, I must remember that next time we are in the Savoy."

"So, tell me, has the house across from you been sold yet?" enquired Daphne.

"Yes, the new people moved in while we on holiday."

"What are they like?"

"We have not really met them yet," said Penelope hurriedly before Cedric could open his mouth.

"Not met them, but you have been back for a whole week now?"

"They only go out at night," said Cedric ignoring Penelope's glare.

"What are they doing at night?"

"Hunting."

"What kind of hunting do they do at night?" asked Sebastain incredulously.

"Cedric is joking," intervened Penelope quickly.

"Perhaps they are ghost hunters," mocked Sebastian.

"We have a ghost" claimed Daphne.

"We don't have any ghosts?" rebuked Sebastian.

"Not here, at mummy's, the ghost of Sir Archibald Thorndyke roams the manor at night."

"Tell us all about him," said Penelope eager to get off the topic of the new neighbours.

"If you're going to talk about ghosts, I'm going to smoke my pipe in the study," said Sebastian.

"What a wonderful idea, why don't you join Sebastian, Cedric?"

"I don t smoke a pipe."

"Come along, Cedric," said Sebastain getting up. "You can see my new cabinet, a real antique."

Penelope gestured for Ceric to follow as she scowled at him.

"Very well," he replied getting up apathetically and trudging after Sebastian.

"A genuine Chippendale," continued Sebastain as they disappeared from the room. "Guess how much?"

Penelope listened to the study door closing.

"Now that they have gone, how are you and Sebastian getting along, Daphne?"

"Well, um, alright I suppose."

"Come on Daphy, I can tell something is up."

"Everything is fine except…"

"Except?"

"Well, in the bedroom, I think he's getting bored of me."

"What makes you say that?"

"Well, he hardly ever wants to, you know, do it."

"Oh, Daphy, you poor thing, sounds like you need to spice things up."

"How?"

"Have you tried wearing sexy lingerie, maybe black stockings and suspenders with a lace negligee?"

"I tried but the suspender strap kept releasing and springing up when I moved."

"You could try holdups. And how about skimpy knickers, maybe a sexy thong?"

"I tried that too but that thin strip is very uncomfortable."

"You could try dressing up and role playing."

"Like what?"

"Whatever you like, teacher and naughty schoolgirl?"

"I'm not sure that's my kind of thing, I never was very good at amateur dramatics. I'll need to think of something soon though."

"I think Daphne should get a job, Cedric," said Sebastian.

"Daphy? Get a job? She doesn't even like mucking out the stables."

"All she does is go riding and attend society functions."

"Sounds good to me," said Cedric conscious that he and Penelope did exactly the same thing. "Besides she doesn't need to work, she has her trust allowance from her mother, Lady Thorndyke."

"Not for the money, it would give her something worthwhile to do with her life. Look at me, I have made enough money to never work again but every day I get up and go into the City. Look here's my business card."

Cedric looked at it, *Sebastian Cornwallis, Financier.*

"You can keep that,"

"Thanks, Sebastian," said Cedric looking around discretely for a bin. ""What sort of job could Daphy do?"

"Anything, she's getting bored, Cedric ,I think a job could be the solution."

(Cedric and Penelope arrive back outside their house)

"We must remember to put the clocks back an hour," said Penelope as they got out of the taxi, feeling the cold night air chill her face. "Oooo it's chilly."

"I'll do my watch right now. Let's see, good lord, it's 3am!" said Cedric as the taxi drove off. "Soon fix that, there we go 2am, that's a bit better."

"Stop playing with that Cedric and let's get inside."

"Where did I put my keys?" said Cedric ferreting in his jacket pockets.

"Hurry up, I'm freezing," said Penelope lifting her hands to her mouth and breathing on them while she rubbed them together vigorously.

"Maybe I left them at Daphy's."

"Cedric, you always do this. It will be in your waistcoat pocket."

"Ah, yes, here it is."

Penelope rushed inside as Cedric turned around and looked at a car turning into the street. The bright headlights illuminated the trees along the verge as it approached. It turned into the drive opposite and stopped. Cedric watched from the porch with curiosity. In the dim light he could just about make out the doors open and the couple get out. Two shadowy figures walked slowly to the front door. As it opened the hall light shone on the couple and Cedric could see them more clearly, albeit from the back. The man was tall and thin, dressed in a black suit, his black hair swept back so it covered his collar. The woman beside him was almost the same height in her high stiletto heels that protruded below a flowing black dress. She was incredibly slim, made even more so by the belt around the middle and the long, lank, blood red hair that extended down below her waist. As she went inside the man suddenly turned around, Cedric froze, unable to move as he looked at his sunken, lifeless eyes and pale, gaunt skin stretched over his bony face. He smiled at him before spinning rapidly, disappearing and closing the door. Cedric remained motionless looking at the closed door. The street was eerily silent, the house opposite cast once more into darkness. He felt an icy gust cut through his body making him shudder. As he hurried inside he made a mental note to buy some garlic.

SCENE 3

CEDRIC AND PENELOPE'S HOUSE

THE FOLLOWING MORNING

"That's it, I'm getting a cross for the front door."

"You are being ridiculous, Cedric."

"I saw them last night, definitely vampires. What do you think they were doing out so late?"

"Could be anything, returning home from work?"

"What work finishes at 2am?"

"Lots, bars, night clubs, factory jobs, fast food outlets."

"What, so they work in McDonald's?"

"Or they could be coming home after a party."

"Looking like Gomes and Morticia Adams?"

"Might have been a fancy dress party, it's almost Halloween."

"What were they wearing when you saw them last week?"

"I can't be expected to remember what people wear, Cedric."

"I bet it they were wearing black, a black suit and a black flowing dress."

"Now that you mention it I think it was, I only saw them very briefly."

"Did you see her red hair, that's to conceal any blood that spurts up when she bites someone's neck."

"You are letting your imagination run wild, Cedric."

"Look, all their curtains are still closed and it's almost 12," said Cedric peeking through the window.

"Probably still in bed."

"They don't sleep in beds."

"They were up late last night."

"It looks unnaturally quiet to me, Penelope," said Cedric continuing to stare out of the window.

"It all looks normal to me," said Penelope approaching and glancing out. "I see they have a package."

"Where?"

"It's behind their car, you can just see the edge of the box sticking out by the bumper."

"I wonder what it is."

"Come away from the window, Cedric," said Penelope moving back. "It's none of our business."

"We could make it our business."

"What do you mean?"

"Go over and see what it is," said Cedric crossing the lounge.

"You cannot go poking at other people's property," said Penelope following him into the hall.

"Why not, they're asleep or whatever state they are in before dark, besides vampires are not really people."

"And what if they are not asleep and catch us?"

"Good point, Penelope, do we have any wooden stakes?"

"What if other neighbours see us, it's not going to look good."

"We'll just pretend we are welcoming the new neighbours. Are you coming?

"Alright, but just to look."

"Great," said Cedric opening the front door. "I'll bring a cross, just in case."

The street was quiet as they crossed to the house opposite, Behind the car they studied the long rectangular object covered in beige cardboard.

"What do you think it is, Cedric?"

"It's got to be over seven feet long and about two feet in height and width."

"A sideboard?"

"Where's the legs?"

"Perhaps they are inside and you have to attach them yourself. Like IKEA."

"I don't think it's from IKEA," mused Cedric kneeling down beside it.

He tapped his knuckles firmly on top.

"It's solid, feels like wood."

" Some sort of cabinet?" said Penelope crouching down on the other side of the package.

"No, I don't think so."

"There's a label here; for D. Mocanu and then the address."

"Strange name."

"Sounds eastern European."

"Romanian?"

"Perhaps."

"Anything else on the label."

"Looks like a return address but it's torn, all I can make out is the word "Mures." Must be foreign, there is a little curl below the "S"."

"Let me see," said Cedric moving around and reading the label.

"Probably aa eastern European language."

"So, we have a long wooden box of some kind sent from somewhere in Eastern Europe to people who have an eastern European name."

They stood up and looked at the package, then at the house with all the curtains drawn and finally at each other.

(Back inside Cedric and Penelope's house)

"It's not a coffin, Cedric."

"Let's look at the facts, Penelope. It was over seven feet long and about two feet in height and width. Also it was made of wood."

"We do not know for certain it was made of wood."

"I think it was wood."

"Even if it was that does not prove anything. I still say it's a sideboard or cabinet."

"Let's look at where it's from. The label had the word "Mures" on it."

"With that little curl under the "S"."

"I'll do a search on the laptop," said Cedric typing. "I'll ignore the curl under the "S." There's a Mures county in Romania. It says. *Mures County is a county of Romania, in the historical region of Transylvania, with the administrative centre in Targu Mures.* See I told you, it's from Transylvania, probably a coffin containing soil..

That's what they do, sleep in coffins containing soil from the motherland.

"You are being ridiculous, Cedric. Maybe they are from there and having belongings delivered."

"I bet they are from Transylvania, probably born there hundreds of years ago. What was the name on the package, Mechanic, or something like that?"

"Mocanu."

"Can you remember how it was spelled?" asked Cedric, his hands eagerly hovering above the keyboard.

"M-O-C-A-N-U."

"Right, let's see. Some singer called Dani Mocanu."

"The package was addressed to D. Mocanu, perhaps it's him. Could be some music equipment."

"No, that's definitely not the chap I saw last night. This Dani Mocanu is far too young and alive looking. Our man is probably named Dracula Mocanu. I'll scroll down. Ah, here we go, *Mocanu surname origin and meaning*. I'll click on the link. It says *The Mocanu surname derives from the Romanian word mocan, meaning inhabitant of the mountainous regions, especially Transylvania.* What did I tell you, Penelope."

"So, their name originates in Transylvania," conceded Penelope looking over his shoulder at the screen. "Look, there are 44.000 people with the surname Mocanu in Romania, 1,300 in Spain, even 150 in England, Are you saying they are all vampires?"

"They didn't all just have a coffin delivered from Transylvania."

"It is not a coffin, Cedric. And even if it was, what do they want it for?"

"To sleep in during the day."

"So, what have they been sleeping in until now?"

"Good point, Penelope," said Cedric reclining back and scratching his chin.

"And why is there only one?"

"I have it, they already have their own coffin and this is an extra one."

"For whom?"

"Their next victim."

ACT II

SCENE 1

IN THE TOWN CENTRE

THE FOLLOWING AFTERNOON

"Just look at these fresh tomatoes, Cedric. There are so few authentic greengrocers about now."

"Put this in the basket too."

"You know garlic always gives you bad breath."

"It's not for eating. I wonder if they have any mustard seeds."

"What do you want with mustard seeds?"

"Apparently, you sprinkle them on the roof to keep vampires away."

"Where did you get that crazy idea?"

"I read it on the internet."

"Where on the internet?"

"Some vampire site."

"Cedric, you have to stop looking at these ridiculous sites. There is no such thing as vampires."

"Except the Mocanus."

"They are not vampires, Cedric," said Penelope putting the garlic back on the shelf. "Let's pay for the tomatoes and go. I want to get some flowers for grandmother's grave."

"Good, I can get some blackthorn."

Penelope was not asking.

Cedric and Penelope walk along the street in the direction of the florists.

"That coffee shop looks new, Penelope."

"Another international franchise, soon our high street will look exactly the same as every other high street. The same department stores, the same clothes shops, the same fast food places, even the same pubs."

"That's different, I think it's new as well," said Cedric pointing at a building across the street. "Dark Passion Lap Dance Club."

"I do not know who would want to go into a place like that."

"Well, there's one person going in right now. I'm not surprised he has his hat pulled down over his eyes and scarf wrapped over his face, obviously does not want anyone to recognise him."

"I do not think it's a man, look at the long hair tucked into the coat collar."

"Men have long hair too, Penelope."

"Yes, but look at the slender figure, that has to be a woman."

"It's hard to tell with the overcoat and jeans."

"Look at the trainers, those are far too small for a man."

The figure opened the door and lowered the scarf from their face as they entered quickly and disappeared.

"I don't believe it, Cedric. That was Daphne."

SCENE 2

THE CEMETERY

(Cedric and Penelope are walking to the cemetery)

"We are late back due to that train delay, Cedric. It's getting dark already."

"And it's chilly," replied Cedric breathing on his hands.

"What do you think Daphne was doing at that Lap Dance club?"

"Perhaps she likes that sort of thing."

"Daphne? I hardly think so."

"What do you think then?"

"I'm not sure, perhaps she is going for a job there."

"What? As a lap dancer? said Cedric incredulously.

"No, they are bound to have an office. Maybe she is going to do the admin or accounts."

"Sebastian was telling me he thinks she should get a job, maybe he has talked her into it. I'll give her a ring when we get back home and ask her."

"You will do no such thing, Cedric, you will only embarrass her. If she wants to tell us she will. Anyway, this is the entrance to the cemetery, thankfully they have not locked the gate yet. I'll just put these flowers on the grave."

"Can't you do it tomorrow?"

"I might as well do it now as we are here."

"It's pitch black, Penelope."

"I can use my phone as a torch."

"Well, I'm not going into the graveyard in the dark."

"Are you afraid of ghosts?"

"No, vampires."

"Are you still going on about that, there's no such thing as vampires."

"Fine, you go in. I'll wait for you here.

Penelope turned on her phone for light and entered the cemetery.

"Don't be too long," called Cedric as she disappeared into the darkness.

Cedric was so silly, talking about vampires, thought Penelope as she made her way through the gravestones. All the same she had to admit, it was a bit creepy being in the cemetery in the dark, it was so quiet, the only sound she could hear was her own steps crunching the gravel on the path. Cedric was right about the cold, she could feel the icy wind on her face. Her grandmother's grave should be just a bit further along. Suddenly she heard footsteps coming in the opposite direction. She stopped abruptly and shone her light towards them. The tombstones illuminated along both sides of the path but she could not see anyone. She started walking again increasing her speed. Again she heard the gravel being crunched up ahead.

"Hello," she called. "Is anyone there?"

Her voice carried through the stillness but there was no reply.

She shone the light all around. Nothing but gravestones. Then she noticed a stone cross, perched on top was the blackest raven she had ever seen. The bird watched her with its piercing eyes. Without warning it gave a bloodcurdling screech as it spread its wings and took off. Penlope jumped back in fright causing the light to fall to the ground and extinguish casting everything into darkness. She knelt down and scrambled about, running her hands over the gravel. Then she could hear the footsteps again.

"Hello?" she called as she scoured the ground frantically for the phone.

The gravel crunched louder as the footsteps drew ever nearer.

"Cedric? Is that you?

She felt a bony hand grip her shoulder.

SCENE 3

CEDRIC AND PENELOPE'S HOUSE

THE FOLLOWING DAY

"I knew it, now we are all doomed. I knew it was a bad idea going into the cemetery at night. Now look what's happened."

"Cedric, you are over reacting, the Mocanus are just coming to dinner."

"Now that we have invited them in they will be able to enter the house anytime they want, that's a rule with vampires."

"They are not vampires, actually, they are a very nice couple. They helped me to find my phone last night and introduced themselves, her name is Adelina and his is D…"

"Dracula?"

"Darius," said Penelope glaring at him.

"What were they doing in the graveyard anyway?"

"They have relatives who are buried there."

"Well, all I can say is I hope they stay buried."

"That's a terrible thing to say, Cedric."

"That coffin they had delivered is for somebody."

"It's not a coffin."

"What is it then? Did you ask them?"

"No, I did not, and you are not to either."

"Are they from Transylvania?"

"I never asked them, Cedric. Although they did have a thick eastern European accent. You can ask them tonight."

"They are coming tonight?"

"Yes."

"You could have at least invited them to lunch."

"I did originally but they are busy in the afternoon."

"Sleeping?"

"Right, I'm going to start preparing dinner for tomorrow night," said Penelope ignoring him.

"Remember to add lots of garlic."

"We are not having garlic. What are you going to do?"

"More research on vampires."

ACT III

SCENE 1

CEDRIC AND PENELOPE'S HOUSE

THE DINNER

A loud knock at the door.

"That will be them. Cedric, are you ready."

Cedric comes down the stairs into the hall.

"Why have you got that thick scarf wrapped around your neck?"

"I'm not taking any chances."

"Take it off, you look ridiculous. And what is that on your jumper?"

"A sprig of blackthorn, it keeps away v…"

"Don't say it," interrupted Penelope. "I do not want to hear any of that talk while they are here. I want them to feel welcome, take it off too."

Cedric sullenly removed the blackthorn and unravelled the scarf to reveal a turtle neck pulled up to his chin. Penelope sighed heavily and rolled her eyes.

"Just open the door and remember what I said."

Cedric opened the door.

"Welcome to our home," said Penelope.

Cedric studied them both warily. He seemed even taller up close and thinner in his black suit. The light reflected off his jet black hair. She was wearing a striking black dress that exposed her bare shoulders. Long hair came down below a thin belt around her slim waist. Her rouge lipstick contrasted against her pale skin and the mascara around her eyes made them piercing like a hawk.

"Come in, come in," invited Penelope smiling warmly..

"Thank you," he said stepping over the threshold.

No going back now thought Cedric.

"Darius Mocanu," he said introducing himself to Cedric. "And this is my wife Adelina."

He extended his hand. Cerdric looked at the long, bony fingers and sharp nails before moving his own hand forward. Darius took it firmly, Cedric noted how cold it was, almost like ice, probably just got out of his coffin.

"I apologise, my hand must be very cold, it is very, as you say, chilly tonight.

"I told you wear gloves, Darius, you are never listening to me," admonished Adelina, her voice shrill. "We brought you this."

She held out a bottle of red wine, at least Cedric hoped it was wine. He stood transfixed studying the crimson liquid through the dark green glass.

"I hope you like it," said Darius. "We brought it from Romania."

"That's very kind of you," said Penelope taking the bottle. "Come into the lounge. Cedric put the wine in the kitchen and open the Chateau Mouton."

She handed him the bottle and they went into the lounge while Cedric walked slowly down the hall to the kitchen still examining the bottle and wondering where he could get the contents analysed. Best not to tell Penelope, he thought, as he placed the bottle in the wine rack and removed the Chateau Mouton.

"Just sit anywhere," invited Penelope.

The couple sat side by side on the sofa.

"How are you settling in?"

"It is very nice here, but we have much to do," replied Adelina.

"Oh, yes. it's always very hectic when one moves house. Cedric and I will have been here ten years come next March. The neighbours are nice enough, mostly older with conservative almost Victorian values."

"What is meaning Victorian values?"

"Well, they do not like any scandal or trouble," clarified Penelope who had no intention of telling them about Mrs. Fotheringham and the peeping Tom incident."

Adelina looked at Darius and raised her eyebrows.

"It's very quiet and ordinary here, quite boring really," added Penelope.

"That is why we chose this area," said Darius as Cedric entered carrying a tray of wine. "We wanted a quiet and peaceful place."

Cedric stood stock still, what did he mean by a peaceful place? Somewhere they would not be disturbed while they roamed the streets at night collecting bodies?

"Let me help you," said Penelope taking two glasses from the tray and handing them to the visitors.

Cedric watched as Darius raised the glass to the mouth and the red liquid touched his lips, his eyes lighting up as he drank. As he lowered the glass a thin red line trickled from the side of his mouth.

"Oh, excuse me," he said quickly wiping it away. "The wine is most exquisite."

"Delightful, " purred Adelina.

"I do not think I have had this wine before," assessed Darius. "I am thinking it is a Bordeaux, maybe a Cabernet Sauvignon blend."

"Are you a connoisseur, Darius?" asked Penelope.

"I would not say a connoisseur but we like, especially the reds. In Romania we favour the Feteasca Neagra wines."

"Is that where you are from?"

"Yes. a small town called Targu Mures>"

"Transylvania," blurted Cedric.

"Ah, you know Romania?"

"Well, no, not exactly."

"How do you know Targu Mures? It is very small, most English people only know Bucharest."

"I read it somewhere," he said hastily.

"We are not actually living in Targu Mures," clarified Adelina. "Rather in a remote area to the north of the town."

"In a castle?"

Penelope glared at Cedric through narrowed eyes.

Darius and Adelina looked at each other.

Time seemed to stand still as silence descended like a heavy veil.

Cedric knew he had said too much, they would have no choice now but to kill them and turn them into vampires. Thank heavens he wore his turtle neck.

Darius roared with laughter.

"I am thinking you are reading too much fiction. No one in Transylvania lives in a castle."

"Cedric was just joking," said Penelope hurriedly.

"Ah, you having fun with us, very good."

"I think we can sit at the table and I will serve dinner."

Cedric sat at the head of the table while Darius and Adelina sat on either side facing each other.

"I hope you like Roast Beef and Yorkshire Pudding, I thought I would make a traditional English meal," said Penelope wheeling in a trolley from the kitchen.

"We have not tried before," said Adelina. "But it looks wonderful."

Penelope served the food and sat opposite Cedric.

"Wonderful," complimented Darius as he savoured the meat and gravy.

"It is customary to have it with English mustard but we appear to have run out," said Penelope.

"I have some mustard seeds," said Cedric incurring another scowl from Penelope.

"What dishes do you normally eat in Romania?" she enquired.

Cedric resisted the temptation to say blood pudding of dubious provenance.

"Sarmale is very popular," said Adelina.

"What is that?"

Blood pudding?

"A type of cabbage roll."

Cedric made a mental note never to go to a Romanian restaurant.

"It is filled with…"

Blood?

"…pork, bacon, rice, onion and tomato juice."

Or something that looks like tomato juice.

"It is very popular in Romania."

"Well, it sounds delicious," said Penelope.

"I will make it for you to try. You can come to our house."

During the day, right?

"That sounds divine. So, what brings you to England?

Adelina looked at Darius with uncertainty. Cedric sat upright eagerly awaiting the response.

"We were forced to leave Romania," said Darius.

Chased out with pitchforks?

"Our business had problems, so we decided to continue our affairs here."

"What line if business are you in?"

Adelina remained silent, Darius lifted his glass slowly to his lips and took a long sip. Cedric's eyes opened wide as he leant forward.

"Entertainment," said slowly and deliberately.

What entertainment? Their entertainment at hunting people for sport?

The table fell silent, Penelope could sense an uneasiness.

"What is Romania like?" she asked hastily.

"Where we lived was very nice. We had the wonderful green scenery of the Carpathian hills. And Targu Mures and the surrounding villages were very safe, we never lock our doors, no-one really does."

Bad news for the villagers.

"Do you lock your doors at night" asked Adelina.

"Yes!" said Cedric rather too loudly. "All doors and all windows, a triple lock on the front door and a chain and…"

He was stopped by a kick in the shins under the table.

"Just the way we were brought up in England. This is a very safe area," said Penelope.

Until now, thought Cedric reaching down and rubbing his leg.

****

"You've bruised my shin," said Cedric sitting in the armchair after the guests had departed with his trouser leg rolled up to his knee.

"That's because you were being rude to Darius and Adelina, Cedric, I thought they were a very nice couple. I hope you are going to drop this notion about them being vampires now just because they come from Transylvania."

"They were very cagey about telling us what their business was."

"Well, that is really none of our concern. I'm going to bed, are you coming?

"I'll just double check all the doors are locked."

Penelope sighed audibly and shook her head as she went out into the hall.

Cedric wondered where he could get a big dog.

SCENE 2

BACK IN THE TOWN CENTRE

THE FOLLOWING WEEK

"It should be a good show this evening, Cedric, we have not been to the theatre in ages."

"We can eat in that little restaurant around the corner from the theatre."

"That reminds me, I thought Darius and Adelina might have invited us back for dinner by now."

"No doubt they will soon enough and we'll be the dinner."

"Now that I think about it I have not seen them since last week."

"Well, you wouldn't, would you, I told you they only come out after dark."

"I quite fancied trying their filled cabbage rolls."

"Really, I'd rather have anything other than cabbage rolls,"

"You are so unadventurous, Cedric."

"I just like what I like and I don't like cabbage."

"It's good for you."

"So is jogging but I'm not doing that either."

"There's that lap dancing club. Do you suppose Daphne is inside working in the office? We could always go in and ask for her."

"It might not have been her that we saw last week, Penelope. It was starting to get dark."

"It definitely was Daphne, I would know her anywhere. Just like I know that that is Sebastian."

"Where?"

"On the other side of the street, just going past the shoe shop. Sebastian!" called Penelope waving her hand.

"He's certainly moving, I wonder where he's going in such a hurry."

"I don't think he's seen us, let's cross the road. Sebastian!"

Sebastian stopped and looked at them approaching.

"Have you seen, Daphne," he asked frantically.

"Not since last week," said Penelope. "Why?"

"She's gone missing."

"What do you mean missing?"

"She didn't come home last night."

"Probably stayed with her mother up at the manor."

"No, they she has not seen her."

"Maybe she is busy," said Cedric looking at the lap dance club.

"Doing what?"

"Maybe she got a job?"

"In the evening? Doing what?"

"Maybe it's a surprise. You said she should get a job."

Sebastian looked at him incredulously.

"Let me know if you see her. I've got to go back to the office."

(Back in their street)

"Another train cancellation, Penelope, the railway service is getting worse and worse, thank goodness the last train was still running."

"I know, it's gone midnight. Somebody else is getting home late."

"Who?"

"Those three up ahead."

"I wonder who that is. Do you recognise them?"

"No, they are too far away."

"They are turning into the house opposite ours."

"Must be Darius and Adelina, Cedric."

"Who is that with them? Come on," urged Cedric speeding up.

"I can see the door opening."

"Quick, before they go inside," he said almost breaking into a run.

"Hold on, Cedric, I can't run in these shoes."

The light from the hall shone momentarily on the group before the door closed leaving the house in darkness.

"Did you see who was with them, Penelope?"

"Yes, that was Daphne."

SCENE 3

CEDRIC AND PENELOPE'S HOUSE

"We have to save Daphne, Penelope, I only hope we are not too late."

"We don't know why she is there, Cedric. It could all be very innocent."

"Why is she there after midnight?"

"I do not know, perhaps they have all been out together and have come back for a nightcap."

"Does she know the Mocanus?"

"She never mentioned them."

"And why did she not tell Sebastian where she was going?"

"I do not know. Cedric, do you really think they are vampires?"

"It would explain that new coffin we saw delivered."

"Oh Cedric. We have to do something."

"We will,"

Cedric took the broom from the storage room, snapped the brush off and broke the pole in two. Then he went into the kitchen and chopped the ends into sharp points with the meat cleaver.

"We'll need these stakes," he said handing one to Penelope. "Ok, let's go."

They went out into the dark, quiet street and moved quickly across the road and up the gravel driveway.

"Look, there's a light on in the lounge, Cedric. What do you think they are doing?"

"Probably performing some sort of satanic ritual. We might be just in time. I'll need to kick the door down or break a window to get in."

"No, you will not need to. They told us they never lock their doors, remember."

"Ah-ha, they have made a mistake."

They crept up to the front door. Cedric put his hand on the handle and turned it slowly and silently. Then he pushed it gently and it opened gradually into the dimly lit hall. They could hear faint piano music coming from the end.

"The ceremony must have started," whispered Cedric tightening his grip on the stake.

They moved stealthily along the passageway, the music getting louder, Cedric leading and Penelope just behind. At the end of the passage they stopped at the closed door, they could see a flickering light at the foot.

"Ready," mouthed Cedric.

Penelope nodded and lifted her stake.

Cedric exhaled heavily and lowered his hand to the knob raising the stake above his head. The door creaked as it opened. Cedric remained motionless and listened. The music was louder through the ajar door. He continued to open it, the creaking less marked. They stepped softly into the L-shaped room. At the back they could see a candelabra on top of a grand piano illuminating Darius who sat playing, oblivious to their presence. Abruptly the music stopped.

"Do it now," instructed Darius.

"STOP!"

Cedric and Penelope rushed around the corner, stakes lifted threateningly.

At the end of the angulation was a slightly raised stage. Two metal poles stood side by side attached to the floor and ceiling.

Wrapped around each pole in tight lycra was Adelina and Daphne. To the side of the stage they could see a long wooden crate. Written on the side in large, bold letters were the words *dance poles*.

Penelope lowered her stake and sighed. She looked at Cedric and shook her head.

"Penelope! Cedric! What are you doing here?" exclaimed Daphne getting off the pole.

"We saw you come in," mumbled Cedric." And, um…"

"You discovered my secret. I was slightly worried when I saw you outside Darius's club last week. I didn't know if you had seen me or not, I guess you had."

"It's your club?" said Cedric turning towards Darius.

"Yes, we did not want to tell you."

"Why ever not?"

"Well, a lot of people disapprove of that sort of thing. So, after you told us that this area is very conservative with, how did you describe it, "Victorian values," we thought it best not to say. We were concerned you might be one of these people."

"So, you see, I'm learning to pole dance," said Daphne.

"For a job?" asked Cedric dumbfounded.

"No, to spice up her marriage," speculated Penelope. "Right, Daphy?"

"Exactly. Adelina gives private lessons for those who want to learn. I did not want anyone to know, especially Sebastian, that's why I sneaked away without telling him. This is my final rehearsal so I can surprise him."

"He was worried about you," said Cedric.

"I'm sorry, but it was the only way I could think of doing it in secret. Darius is going to drive me home tonight."

"Why did you get the poles from Romania?" asked Cedric.

"There is a very good manufacturer in Targu Mures who makes excellent quality poles," replied Darius. "How did you know they were from Romania?"

"Umm."

"What are you doing with those sticks" asked Daphne.

Cedric and Penelope looked at each other and started laughing.

"It's a long story."

THE ROOM

"Get the torches, the storm has knocked out the electrics."

The wind lashed ferociously through the bars and onto the windows, made even louder and more terrifying in the darkness. Inside the wailing grew louder as the storm intensified. Beams suddenly appeared in the passageway illuminating the deranged face of a man in a light blue gown.

"Get him back in his room."

The man in the gown was grabbed roughly and dragged down the passage as another figure appeared.

"The storm has knocked out the electronic doors."

"I said it was a bad idea to run everything electronically, this was an accident waiting to happen."

"Just lock all the doors manually before anymore get out, And check everyone is here."

"What about the main entrance?"

"I'll check it myself, give me a torch."

He raced along the corridor into the foyer feeling the powerful gusts that caused his white jacket to flap wildly behind him. The large oak door was slamming violently against the wall. He fought his way to the entrance and shone the light out through the driving rain. On the lawn he could see the deep imprint of fresh footsteps just below the sign Meadowbank Sanitarium.

The rain pelted mercilessly off the ground and the wind rustled through the trees with a ferocity that caused them to bend. Even the thick trunked oaks shuddered as they struggled to stay rooted. In the distance thunder rumbled ominously. A forked lightning bolt crashed from the thick black clouds momentarily illuminating the figure of a young woman struggling along the path, long bedraggled hair swept over her face, her gown flapping violently. Another lightning bolt lit up the night sky and an old house on the hill. She looked up through the driving rain and scrambled to ascend. Her canvas shoes were completely soaked as she splashed through the rapidly forming puddles. The ceaseless wind forced her from side to side, almost bringing her to her knees but a steely resolve drove her forward until she reached the door. She rattled the handle but in was locked. To the side was a small window. She ran her hand over the ground until she found a large rock, using it to smash the glass. The storm raged all around her. She took off her shoe and used it to knock away the shards before scrambling through the small opening.

In the sanitarium the lights flickered and came back to life illuminating the foyer. The orderly ran down the passageway.

"The electrics are back but we've got one missing>"

"Who?"

"Marianne Westlake."

"Notify the police.

The orderly nodded and turned.

"Warn them that she is extremely dangerous. Both to herself and others."

Inside the house the young woman ran her hands along the walls until she located the switch. She flicked it down and a naked bulb hanging by a cable in the centre of the ceiling illuminated the room and she found herself in a small, dank kitchen. She looked around at the rusted sink and the counters caked in dust. There were two wooden cabinets, one with the door drooping down from its broken hinges. The tiles on the floor were dirty and several broken or missing completely. A tall grubby fridge freezer stood in the corner. It looked like it had once been white but now was grey. The bottom door was open revealing an empty freezer compartment. She opened the fridge door. There was no light and no coldness within only a small block of cheese covered in green mould. The stench reached her nostrils making her retch and she quickly closed the door. Her stomach rumbled and her eyes darted about the kitchen. She moved desperately to the cabinets and yanked open the loose door with such force that it detached from the hinge and crashed against the tiles. It contained nothing but dust and gunge. She ripped open the other door and beamed with delight, reaching to the back and pulling out a small cylindrical tin. The label was torn but she could see the picture of a fish and part of a word, *una*. She pulled open the drawer above. Scattered inside were a few items of cutlery. She took out the fork with a bent prong before opening the second drawer. Inside was a sparse selection of utensils: a ladle, a spatula a peeler and a large carving knife. She picked up the carving knife. Placing the tip of the blade on the top of the tin she hit the end of the handle hard, driving it into the metal. She did it again and again around the circumference then cut between the holes until she was able to prise open the jagged top. The tuna was a healthy pink in the brine and smelled exquisite to her. She plunged the fork into the meat and ate hungrily. The food was gone in seconds. Outside the wind raged through the broken window causing her to shiver and become aware of the water dripping from her drenched clothes. At the other side of the kitchen she could just about make out a hallway though the darkness and a staircase. The thunder rumbled louder, drawing ever nearer. She picked up the carving knife and proceeded into the hallway towards the stairs.

She flicked the switch to light up the bare, wooden staircase, It creaked as she ascended slowly, the knife held firmly out in front. On the landing were two closed doors opposite each other and a metal spiral staircase that led to the apex of the house. She looked at the door on the right and trembled, retreating until her back was against the other door, her hand tightening on the knife. Her heart was beating fast and her breathing was rapid and uneven. She closed her eyes and tried to compose herself. She reminded herself she was safe now. Her heart slowed and her breathing returned to normal. She turned to face the room behind. A rectangular plate hung from a nail in the middle with a picture of a pony. She looked at it and smiled before opening it. The room was small, a thin single bed rested against the back wall. The sheets were grubby and stained with faded red spots. A torn pillow with feathers bulging from the rips was strewn against the iron headboard. She moved closer and saw a knotted rope tied to either side. The sight sent a chill down her spine. On the other side of the room was a small circular seated vanity chair with a high back. It was situated in front of an old wooden dressing table with a large vertical mirror attached to the back covered in dust. She sat in the chair and wiped her hand across the dusty mirror and looked at her reflection. Her hair was matted across her face. She swept the bedraggled, wet hair away and smiled weakly. It had been a long time. She looked at the flaked, silver candelabra beside the mirror and shuddered. The candles were almost down to the metal, a few matches lay scattered below, some little more than black ash, but some unused. She put her hands on the small brass handles on the front of the dressing table. The drawer was stiff and groaned as it opened jerkily. A few pencils lay scattered inside and on top of a small note pad lay a wooden hairbrush. She took it out and ran her hand along the bristles before combing it through her hair. It got caught on her long strands. She gripped the roots and tugged it, causing some hairs to be pulled out. Clumps of hair were stuck to the brush, Her face hardened. She smashed it violently against the edge of the table causing the head to break from the handle and spin across the floor.

She stood up and moved to the wardrobe turning the rusted key in the lock and opening the doors. Inside a selection of dresses hung from a metal rack. Her eyes sparkled as she ran her hand along them feeling the soft material. She removed an electric blue one and admired it. Moving to the mirror she held it in front of her body and stretched out the sequined sleeve along her arm. It could have been made for her. She placed it over the back of the chair and quickly slipped out of her wet clothes before pulling it over her head. A little tighter than she expected but it felt silky against her skin. She swirled the bottom as she admired herself in the mirror tossing her hair back and smiling. It had been a long time since she had felt this happy. She danced about the room in her bare feet, the hem swaying from side to side as she moved. Abruptly she stopped and looked up at the ceiling. Through the rumbles of distant thunder and the rain beating on the window it sounded like scratching, something scratching on the floorboards above. She listened intensely. The sound had stopped. Had she imagined it? The thunder boomed louder, she moved slowly to the doorway and glanced up the spiral staircase into the darkness at the top. She could just about make out a narrow door. The attic room, she thought. Suddenly she heard the scratching again coming from the room above. She held her breath. The scratching stopped and she heard a thud. What was that? She quickly looked back into the bedroom and the knife on the dressing table. Another thud then another. Footsteps. Somebody was up there.

She returned to the dressing table and picked up the knife. There did not appear to be a light switch for the upper level. She tightened her grip on the knife and put her foot onto the bottom of the spiral staircase. The metal frame creaked and vibrated. She put her hand onto the banister and went slowly up, looking ever upwards into the darkness, the blade of the knife pointing forwards. The rain beat off the roof getting louder as she ascended. At the top on the wall beside the door was a single bulb protruding with a cord below. She pulled it and the bulb lit up the narrow area.

"Hello!" she called facing the door.

No reply.

"Hello!" she shouted louder.

The only sound was the ever persistent rain and wind pounding on the roof above.

She studied the door. It was shabby and a spider's web covered a top corner. Just below it she saw a thick metal bolt locked across the frame. She lifted her hand to it. It was stiff. She placed the knife on the floor and began working it up and down with both hands. The metal squeaked as inch by inch it came out of the lock. She knelt down and picked up the knife before placing her hand on the knob. She twisted it and pulled. The door was locked.

"Hello! Is anybody in there?" she called again.

No reply. Perhaps it had been her imagination. She turned back to the stairs and stopped abruptly. There it was again, the scratching. She returned to the door and placed her ear against the wood. The sound had ceased. She had an idea. Quickly she descended the stairs and went into the bedroom, She opened the drawer, removed the pad and one of the pencils and reascended the stairs. Outside the door she scribbled a note and slid it underneath so half of it was still sticking out. Her eyes remained fixed on the sheet. The thunder roared louder, it was now over the house. Suddenly there was a crash above her as a bolt of lightning struck the roof. The impact cast everything into darkness. She yanked the cord of the light bulb frantically but it was dead. The lower level was equally black. She screamed as another terrifying bolt struck the roof. She felt for the banister and descended tentatively, feeling for each stair with her foot before placing her weight onto it. Slowly and gradually she got to the bottom. It was impossible to see anything in the darkness. Carefully she entered the bedroom with her arms outstretched and felt for the dressing table. She ran her hands across the top until she located the candelabra. She scoured the top for the box of matches and an unused match. Once found she struck it along the side of the box. The flame flicked into life. Steadily she touched it against the wick. The candle illuminated the room. She picked it up and returned to the attic door. The sheet of paper still protruded from underneath. Maybe there was no one there, perhaps it was merely mice. Resignedly she bent down and picked up the paper. There was something written on it.

She looked at her question:

Is anybody in there?, then the response, *I knew you would come.*

She stared wild eyed at the closed door.

"What do you mean? Who are you?" she demanded almost dementedly.

No reply.

"Answer me!"

Nothing.

128

She sat down quickly and placed the candle on the floor, scribbling frantically before sliding it back under. Her push was forceful and the page disappeared underneath. She waited impatiently, listening to the rain rattling against the tiles on the roof and the thunder now roaring. Her eyes darted wildly around the small landing from the gap under the door, to the stairs, to the ceiling. All the while she fidgeted with the knife, twirling it slowly in her hand. She ran a finger along the blade gently feeling its sharpness and bouncing her crossed legs so her knees banged on the floor. Her eyes now fixed on the gap under the door, all seemed silent behind. She bit her lower lip and gently rocked back and forth. As the rocking increased in speed she pressed her finger more firmly onto the blade. Feeling the pain as it cut into her flesh. She removed her finger and held it up to the candle. A thin trail of blood trickled from the incision. She put it in her mouth and tasted it. What was in the room? Agitatedly she plunged the knife hard into the floorboards so the handle stuck up in the air. She scrambled onto her knees and reached under the gap at the bottom of the door, straining her fingertips, until they brushed the paper. She lay on her stomach, feeling the damp wood through the dress. Forcing her hand further under the door, the wood scrapping the skin on top. Her fingers pinched the edge of the paper and she slowly dragged it out. She knelt up, holding it to the candle and reading:

Who are you? and the answer, *You know who I am.*

She grabbed the door knob forcibly with both hands and rattled it frenziedly but it would not budge.

"Let me in!" she screamed.

She released the knob and scribbled agitatedly on the paper, sliding it back under the door. Above she could hear the tiles being ripped off the roof by the increasingly ferocious storm. They crashed to the ground outside as the thunder grew louder and louder. She saw the edge of the paper sticking out and seized it and read.

It is locked from the outside.

Feverishly she scribbled and pushed it back under. Waiting for what seemed an eternity while the storm raged. She tried to look under the door but the room was in darkness. She pulled out the note and read,

Who locked you in and why?

They did it, they said I was a bad girl and must be punished but I punished them.

"What did you do?" she cried wild eyed.

Silence from the other side of the door.

She scribbled feverishly and pushed it back under. She sat agitated brushing her hand through her wet hair over and over again simultaneously wanting and not wanting a response. She grabbed the page.

What did you do?

You know what I did.

No, she did not know, she did not want to know. Of all places why had she come here. Here to this place. She stood up and with wild eyes beat on the door with her fists until her knuckles started to bleed. She turned abruptly and hurried down the stairwell back into the bedroom. In the mirror she could see her reflection. The once pristine dress was now covered in dirt and dust. She yanked the dressing table drawer completely out and tipped it upside down, the contents clattering onto the wooden floor. Throwing herself to the ground she scrambled through the objects. There was no sign of the key. She stood up and flung open the wardrobe, hurling everything out. The driving rain lashed against the window. She looked out into the hall at the closed door of the room opposite, She knew she had to go in. Slowly she got to her feet, the howling wind seemed appropriate as she crossed the hall. For a moment she stood still, just staring at the closed door. She lowered her hand to the knob and turned it gradually, pushing the door open inch by inch. The candlelight threw a shadow around the room onto the bedstead and dressing table. She looked nervously at the floor, lifted her right foot and placed it tentatively inside. With one hand holding onto the door frame she put her other foot in. She was doing it. She walked slowly and deliberately placing one foot at a time. There was no need to be afraid anymore.

She held the candle over the large double bedstead. It was surrounded by four wooden posts that extended to frame above. The sheets were smoothed out and tightly tucked in. Two pillows were puffed up against the headboard, Despite its neatness she could see the film of dust on the wooden frame. She moved to the dressing table, Everything was timelessly in place. Her eyes focused on a small vanity case and she trembled. She undid the clip on the front and lifted the lid. It swung back on its hinges. The inside was empty except for a small metal key. She stood transfixed looking at it, just a key and yet. She scooped it up and rushed back up to the attic.

The thunder bellowed above and the lightning crackled more intensely. She stood before the door with the key in her hand. What would she find inside? She inserted the key into the lock and turned, listening to the lock mechanism. The door swung open and she felt the cold air on her face. The interior was pitch black. She reached up and pressed the light switch she knew would be there but the room remained dark. She picked up the knife and entered.

The ceiling was low and sloped down under the apex. A small metal bed lay below covered by a thin, torn blanket. A cobweb hung from the corner and dust covered the floor. The other half of the dingy room was still in darkness but she could see an outline in the shadows. She lifted the candle and inched her way slowly towards it. Her jaw clenched as she raised the knife. . Suddenly a lightning bolt struck the apex and with a terrifying crash ripped a hole in the roof. The rain drove through the gap beating on the wooden floorboards. She stood defiantly and lifted the knife higher, her knuckles white with the force of her grip. A strong gust of wind rushed through the gaping hole and extinguished the candle. In the darkness a woman screamed.

The sun shone brightly in the clear blue sky and the air was warm and still. Outside the house several police cars were parked beside an ambulance.

"It's pretty bad in there, sir, blood everywhere."

"Does anyone know what happened?"

"There were no witnesses."

Two paramedics emerged from the house and descended from the porch carrying a stretcher covered by a blanket to the ambulance.

"Do we know who the victim was?"

"Her name was Marianne Westlake."

"Isn't this the old Westlake place?"

"Yes, she escaped from the sanitarium last night."

"I remember. She was sent there after she killed her parents."

"They used to lock her in the attic apparently, that's where she was found."

"So, she was murdered."

"I don't think so. Look at this, we found it on the attic floor."

He handed him the paper with the scrawled dialogue.

"It's all in the same hand writing."

CEDRIC'S

CHRISTMAS

Characters

Cedric, thirtysomething socialite

Penelope, Cedric's wife

Daphne, friend of Cedric & Penelope

Sebastian, Daphne's husband

Lady Thorndyke, Daphne's mother

Henderson, Lady Thorndyke's butler

Darius, neighbour of Cedric & Penelope

Adelina, wife of Darius

ACT I

TWO DAYS BEFORE CHRISTMAS

CEDRIC AND PENELOPE'S HOUSE

(Cedric is in the closet under the stairs.)

"What are you doing in there Cedric? You had better not be getting more decorations, we already have more up than Trafalgar Square," said Penelope pushing away a large holly branch dangling from the ceiling.

"I'm not."

"What are you doing in there then?"

"Nothing."

"It's no use looking for your present, I might not even have bought it yet."

"Yes, you have , you always buy it early, Penelope."

"Maybe not this year. Maybe I have decided to wait until Christmas Eve to stop you looking for it."

"You said the same thing last year. Besides, Daphy's present is already wrapped and under the tree."

"Perhaps I have only got Daphne's so far."

"Hmm."

"Come out of there. Even if I have bought it I would not hide it in so obvious a place."

"Ah-ha. So, you have bought it already, I knew it," said Cedric coming out and going into the sitting room.

"I never said that," replied Penelope following.

The sitting room was like a Mecca to Christmas, a huge tree covered in brightly coloured baubles and lights extended to the ceiling. The walls were draped in undulating paper decorations going from corner to corner and silver tinsel was around every picture frame. On the mantlepiece were festive ornaments of reindeers and snowmen and in the centre stood a porcelain statue of a jolly Father Christmas sat in a sleigh surrounded by presents. Cedric approached the tree and picked up a small box wrapped in gold foil paper and tied with red lace into a bow on top and a white label with the words *To Daphne.*

I know you have hidden my present somewhere," he said putting it back. "Give me a clue,"

"No."

"I'll find it anyway."

"You never have in the past."

"This year is going to be different, you're running out of hiding places. Unless you reuse the same one. I'm going down to the basement."

"No, you are not. We are going to Lady Thorndyke's for lunch and she will not appreciate you traipsing dirt through the manor."

"Fine. I'll look when we get back."

They open the front door. Affixed to the outside was a massive plastic reindeer head with the antlers protruding into the porch. As it closed the reindeer's nose lit up bright red and Jingle Bells started playing. The music drew the intention of the neighbours across the street who were just going to their car.

"Ah, that's cute," gushed Adelina. "We should get something for our door, Darius."

"Good idea, what do you suggest, Cedric? Maybe an upside down cross?" he said laughing.

Cedric bent down and pretended to tie his shoe.

"Morning Darius, morning Adelina," greeted Penelope. "Cold this morning."

"Morning Penelope," said Adelina. "Yes, I can see we will have to scrape the ice off the windscreen before we go to the shops. Do you want anything?"

"No, thank you. We are all set for Christmas."

"What about you Cedric?" asked Darius. "Do you need any more stakes?"

"Don't tease him, Darius."

Cedric hurried into the car with Darius's laughter ringing in his ears.

"See you later," said Penelope getting in beside him.

"He always does that," bemoaned Cedric sullenly.

"Well you did think he was a vampire."

"It was an easy mistake to make."

"No it was not, it was a ridiculous notion."

"Well, it was ages ago."

"He's just having fun with you, Cedric. Anyway, lunch at Lady Thorndyke's will take your mind off him."

Cedric started the car and they drove off down the street. Lady Thorndyke always had delicious food and lots of it, he thought as a smile spread across his face. Not to mention the excellent wine.

"Daphne and Sebastian are going too."

Oh no, Sebastian. He would have to endure an afternoon with that big headed show off in his ear.

His smile vanished.

LUNCH AT LADY THORNDYKE'S MANOR

"What do you think of my new shoes, Cedric. Genuine Testoni handcrafted Italian leather."

"Very nice, Sebastain," replied Cedric looking about for someone else to talk to.

"Guess how much."

"I don't know."

"Guess."

"£300."

"More."

"£400."

"£600, the leather is so soft it's like wearing slippers."

"Mulled wine, sirs?"

"Thank you, Henderson," said Cedric delighted to be interrupted.

He held the glass in both hands, feeling it warm his fingers as he watched the steam rising. He lifted it to his lips and took a sip, immediately feeling his insides heating up.

"I made it myself, sirs."

"Exquisite as always, Henderson," praised Cedric. "So rich and smooth."

"That will be the maple syrup, my secret ingredient, one tablespoon, no more, no less."

"Well, it's wonderful," commended Cedric taking another sip.

"Lunch will be served presently if you would like to take your seats in the dining room."

Cedric and Sebastian walked down the hall to the dining room. Lady Thorndyke sat at the head of the table with Daphne and Penelope to her left.

"Sebastain, come and sit beside me," invited Lady Thorndyke. "You can give some investment advice."

Sebastian took the seat to her right while Cedric sat beside him.

"I do so love Christmas," gushed Daphne. "Do you still have that reindeer head with the red nose that lights up and plays Jingle Bells, Cedric?"

"Pride of place on the front door, Daphy."

"I do wish you would not refer to her as Daphy, Cedric," admonished Lady Thorndyke. "Her name is Daphne. If I had wanted to name her Daphy I would have had her christened as such."

"Oh, mummy, it's just a pet name, a term of endearment. Cedric has always called me that since we were children. Isn't that right, Cedric?"

"Quite right, Daphy-ne, Daphne," corrected Cedric under the icy glare of Lady Thorndyke.

" Have you got your decorations up, Daphne?" asked Penelope hurriedly.

"Oh, yes, you know me, the house has been decorated since the end of November."

"Way too early, Daphne," complained Sebastian. "And that tree is too big, the branch at the top is scratching all the ceiling."

"You are too grouchy, Sebastian. I am fully expecting you to be visited by three ghosts on Christmas Eve."

"You go over the top, Daphne. Do you know we have a six foot Father Christmas in the garden? It took two men from Harrods to carry in from the van."

Cedric wondered if they would have any left.

"You should embrace the festive spirit, Sebastian. Do you know he stops watching The Grinch after he steals Christmas and considers that a happy ending."

"All I'm saying is that you could tone it down a bit. I would be the laughing stock of The City if they knew I had a six foot Santa in my garden."

"Shall I serve the soup, your ladyship?"

"Yes, please do, Henderson."

"I much prefer the name Father Christmas to Santa Claus," said Daphne as Henderson went around the table filling the bowls from the silver tureen.

"He's based on St. Nicholas," said Sebastian as though he was proclaiming the meaning of life.

"I know that but why on him?"

"He must have gone about giving presents to people at Christmas time."

"He was a monk who lived in the ancient country of Lycia, modern day Turkey," said Penelope. "He gave away most of his money and roamed the countryside helping the poor and sick. In the best known story about him he saved three poor sisters by giving them a dowry so they would not be forced into prostitution."

"I hardly think that is a suitable topic for the dinner table, Penelope," said Lady Thorndyke disapprovingly.

"Sorry, Lady Thorndyke. Lovely soup, Henderson."

"Thank you, ma'am."

"I find it fascinating," said Daphne enthralled. "Go on, Penelope."

"Well, the name Santa Claus comes from of the Dutch for St. Nicholas, Sint Nikolaas, which is shortened to Sinter Klass, hence Santa Claus.

"You are so knowledgeable, Penelope. You were the same at school."

"I just came across an article about it in a magazine. There was a really good piece in it about Edgar Allan Poe."

"So, he had nothing to do with giving out presents at Christmas."

"Apparently not."

"Did he at least have a white beard and wear a red suit?" asked Daphne hopefully.

"I do not think so."

"You are being silly, Daphne," reproached Lady Thorndyke. "Nobody would walk around in a red suit with jingle bells on his boots."

"Quite right, Lady Thorndyke," added Sebastian. "There is no such thing as Santa Claus or Farther Christmas.

"That's disappointing," murmured Daphne looking down at her soup. "I think the world would be a nicer place if there was."

"He may not physically exist but the belief in the concept of Father Christmas is very real," said Penelope.

Daphne looked up and smiled at her affectionately.

"Shall I serve the main course, my lady?"

"Yes, please do, Henderson."

"Talking of Christmas presents, have you found yours yet, Cedric?"

"Not yet, Daphy-ne, Daphne, but I will soon."

"You did not find it last year, or the year before that, or, in fact, any year."

"It will be different this year, I know what it is."

"What?"

"A watch."

"It might not be a watch," said Penelope.

"It's definitely a watch, I have been on about it for months. That's why it's hard to find. It's only small."

"Where was it hidden last year?" asked Daphne. Oh, yes, I remember, in the birdhouse in your garden. That was a clever one. Penelope knows you never take any interest in it."

"I even asked him to feed the birds in the few days before Christmas when the present was in there to give him a hint," said Penelope laughing.

"I'm listening out for any clues this year."

"Perhaps I have given you one already."

"What clue?"

"I'm not telling you. Maybe I have hidden it in the dishwasher and the only way to find it is to empty it."

"Very funny, Penelope."

"Oh, yes, just like that time Penelope left the cord hanging from the attic hatch and you were so convinced it was up there you went up and tidied everything up," gushed Daphne giggling excitedly.

"Ah, here comes the main course," said a relieved Cedric. "What do you have for us, Henderson?"

"Peppered salmon with remoulade and pastis sauce, sir."

"It looks delicious."

"We will have to go shopping tomorrow, Penelope," said Daphne while Henderson served the main course. "I still have a few things to get for Christmas."

"Certainly, Daphne, we can have lunch at the Savoy."

"Delightful, Sebastian is playing golf at his club tomorrow anyway."

"Probably be the last time before Christmas," said Sebastian.

"You could go with Sebastain, Cedric," suggested Penelope.

"I've got plans tomorrow."

"What plans."

Searching the house from top to bottom, and possibly the birdhouse, thought Cedric.

"I have some letters to write."

"To whom?"

"Confidential business."

"Remember you have to put it up the chimney once it's finished," jibed Sebastian.

"Go and play golf with Sebastian," said Penelope. "You could do with the fresh air and it will stop you wasting time looking for your present."

"I wasn't going to do that," lied Cedric.

"Hmm."

"Besides I haven't played golf in years, I don't even know where my clubs are."

"They are in the shed, I saw them a few days ago."

Cedric made a mental note to search the shed.

"What's your handicap, Cedric?" asked Sebastian. "Except your arms."

"I don't have a handicap."

"I myself play off six," announced Sebastian as though he was expecting a round of applause.

"It's settled then," said Daphne. "Penelope and I will go shopping while Sebastian and Cedric play golf."

All day with Sebastian, thought Cedric, can't wait.

ACT II

CHRISTMAS EVE

CEDRIC AND PENELOPE'S HOUSE

Cedric was pacing slowly up and down the sitting room deep in concentration. Penelope had suggested she may have already given him a clue as to the whereabouts of his present which meant she definitely had. She liked to do it right in front of his face so she could refer to it later, she was devious like that. But it would be something cryptic, she would not make it easy for him. There was a good chance it was something said at the lunch yesterday. Now what were they talking about, he pondered. Daphy was talking about Father Christmas and then Penelope told the story of St. Nicholas. Mmm, something to do with St. Nicholas? Cedric could not think of anything they owned that had anything to do with St. Nicholas unless Penelope had hollowed out a book about him and hidden it inside. No, Penelope would never deface a book, she would consider that sacrilege. St. Nicholas, Santa Claus, Father Christmas? That was it. He had it he smiled joyously. He picked up the porcelain statue of Father Christmas on the mantlepiece and turned it upside down looking into the hollow inside. His look of jubilation turned to disappointment, empty.

What else had Penelope said yesterday? Daphne had said how clever she had been at school, always reading. Penelope said she read about St. Nicholas in a magazine and that she had also read another article. What was that about, he thought, racking his brains to remember. Some writer, an old writer, who was it now? Poe, that was it, Edgar Allan Poe. Now what did he write? The Raven. That was it, it was in the birdhouse. Penelope was pulling a double bluff and using the same place as last year, the sly fox. Well, not this time, this year she had tried to be too clever. He replaced the statue as Penelope entered.

"I think it's going to snow, Penelope," said Cedric looking through the window up at the white cloud covered sky. "We won't be able to play golf."

"It is not going to snow, Cedric, it's not cold enough."

"Rain then."

"It is not forecast to rain either, besides you have your waterproof jacket if it does. I am sure you will have a nice time once you get there."

"Hmm."

"You might even win," said Penelope encouragingly.

"I doubt it, he cheats."

"He does not cheat, Cedric."

"Yes, he does, he moves his ball with his foot when he thinks you're not looking."

"Hmm."

"And he is very creative with the score card, knocking strokes off so the score is lower than he really got. He claims his handicap is six, more like 26."

"Do not forget your woolly hat, the wind will be a bit chilly on the course."

Cedric reluctantly put on his hat and traipsed to the door dragging his bag of clubs behind. The birdhouse would have to wait for now.

ON THE GOLF COURSE

"Bloody hell."

Cedric looked at Sebastian outside the club house wearing a bright pink jumper with a white diamond pattern woven around the middle and lemon yellow trousers. He wondered if the circus was back in town.

"Ah, there you are, Cedric. I was beginning to think you had got cold feet after the thrashing I gave you last time."

"You won by one hole after you retook the last tee shot saying you had been distracted by a bird that no-one else saw."

"You can never tell when the little blighters are going to appear."

"Funny how it's normally after you hit a bad shot."

"The usual £10 a hole?" said Sebastian as they walked towards the course.

"Fine" replied Cedric determined to keep a close eye on him.

"Right, I'll tee off, remind you how it's done."

Cedric watched Sebastian's ball disappear into the trees.

"That was just a practice shot," said Sebastian placing a new ball on the tee.

"There's no such thing as a practice shot, you will need to find your ball or drop a shot."

"It's a new club rule, you get a practice shot at the first hole."

It was going to be a long round.

IN TOWN

(Penelope and Daphne are walking down the street carrying bags.)

"I think we have everything Daphne, shall we go back?"

"I want to get something else for Sebastian, something special."

Daphne stopped outside a shop with the name flashing in neon lights in the window.

"Hanky Spanky?"

"Yes."

"A sex shop?"

"I have passed it many times but never had the courage to go in. Have you ever been in?"

"No," said Penelope innocently.

"Shall we go in?"

"I'll wait for you here."

"I don't want to go in by myself, please, please, please."

"Ok, but let's be quick," said Penelope tilting the rim of her hat down to her eyes.

Daphne pushed open the door and entered the dimly lit shop.

"Hi Penelope," greeted the man behind the counter.

"I thought you said you had not been in here before, Penelope?"

"Oh, well, um, I was in once, ages ago."

"He knows your name."

"He must have a good memory."

"Hmm."

"What were you thinking of getting for Sebastian?" said Penelope hurriedly moving down the shop.

"I don't really know," replied Daphne examining a set of fur lined handcuffs. "What do you think of these?"

"Very adventurous, Daphne, have you ever tried bondage?"

"No, have you?"

"No."

"We have a new selection of canes and paddles in, Penelope," said the shop assistant as he passed by with an armful of large, coloured cushions with the word SEX embroidered on them.

"Shall I buy one for Cedric?" asked Daphne. "It sounds like he could do with one."

Penelope laughed and took off her hat.

"I knew you had been in here before, it's always the quiet ones you have to watch. Actually, I'm glad, you can give me the benefit of your expertise."

"I would not describe myself as an expert but happy to help. Do you think Sebastian would look good in a gimp suit?" said Penelope pointing to a full body length black rubber suit hanging from a rail.

"Oh, Penelope, you are awful," said Daphne giggling. "I was thinking of something I could wear."

"You want to wear a gimp suit?"

"Nooo," replied Daphne now laughing uncontrollably drawing looks from other customers.

Penelope harried her deeper into the shop.

"I was thinking of something I could wear, you know, a sexy uniform."

"Oh, they are over here," said Penelope leading the way. "What did you have in mind, a sexy nurse, a sultry teacher, a saucy maid?"

"I always fantasised about being a sexy police woman."

"Excellent choice, here is a police uniform and you can wear it with the handcuffs."

Daphne looked uncertainly at the dark navy uniform that comprised of a peak cap emblazoned with a silver police badge, a short blouse that tied at the front and tight leather shorts.

Penelope took it off the rack and handed it to Daphne.

"There is a changing room at the back. You try it on and I will see what else they have. Maybe a rubber truncheon."

"What do you do with that?"

"I'll explain later."

Despite Sebastian kicking his ball into a better position whenever he thought Cedric was not looking and some, let's say, creative counting, they ended up at the last hole with the scores level, five holes won each and seven drawn. However, both balls were now on the final green with Sebastian having taken three shots while Cedric had taken four. This was in spite of Sebastian hitting his second shot into some thick bushes but it miraculously appearing in a smooth clearing. Cedric was certain it was a different ball that Sebastian had discreetly placed but could not prove it. Fortunately Cedric's ball was closer to the hole but it was still a difficult shot.

"You go first then Sebastian, you are further away."

"I know the rules, Cedric. If I putt this I win as usual."

Cedric knew that.

"I can probably do it in two shots as I cannot see you putting in from that distance."

Cedric knew that too. But he had hope. Sebastian had to hit down the slope, there was always the chance that his ball would roll down too far and even holing with two shots would be difficult.

"Get your money ready, Cedric." he said confidently as he placed the club behind the ball.

It was £10, from the smug smile on his face you would think it was about to win The Open.

He struck the ball and it rolled towards the hole, gathering speed on the slope, shooting past the pin and coming to rest on the bottom edge of the green.

Cedric restrained his laughter.

"I'll still win," said Sebastian, now a lot less assured.

Cedric crouched down behind his ball for a closer look at the line to the hole. It was a long putt, the sort of distance he would not normally make. He stood up, put his club behind the ball and drew it slowly back. Here goes, he thought.

"What's that?" shouted Sebastian suddenly.

Cedric flinched but managed to stop the club before it hit the ball and glared at him.

"Sorry old man, thought I saw a bird."

"Hmm."

"Carry on."

Cedric got ready to play his shot again.

"If you miss I'll probably win."

Cedric ground his teeth.

He concentrated hard, blocking out everything around him and struck. Now every so often Cedric would play a shot that surprised even him, today was such a day. The ball dropped into the hole with a plop.

"You're shot, Sebastian. If you miss I win."

Revenge is a dish best served cold.

Cedric was not sure if it was tension or fury on the face of Sebastian but either way it was joyous.

Sebastian's ball rolled up the slope stopping just before the hole.

"I win," said Cedric cheerily holding out his hand. "£10 please."

Sebastian broke his club.

"What do you think, Penelope?" asked Daphne pulling back the curtain and stepping out of the cubicle.

The little navy blouse exposed a tantalising glimpse of cleavage and her slim, exposed midriff. Her long, chestnut hair cascaded down below the police cap. She turned around to show the small, leather shorts stretched tight across her buttocks.

"You don't think it makes my bum look big, do you?"

"No, very sexy Daphne, you have a lovely small bum."

"Don't get any ideas," said Daphne glancing at the rack of paddles and laughing.

"It will look great with a pair of boots, they keep them over here."

Daphne picked out a pair of black leather high heeled boots that zipped up to just below her knee.

"Fabulous Daphy, that will certainly spice up your marriage."

"I'll just change back and we can go for cocktails at Clarridges before we go home."

Daphne headed for the dressing room while Penelope perused the shelves.

That was a better day than I expected, thought Cedric as he drove home from the golf club in the darkness of the winter's evening. He had seen Sebastian throw a tantrum like a toddler and was £10 up to boot. Even better Penelope would no doubt go for cocktails and not get back until late giving him one last opportunity to find his present.

He entered his street admiring the festive lights in the windows of the neighbouring houses until he arrived at his own. It was lit up like a Las Vegas casino. Every window had coloured lights flashing around the frame and on the roof were more bulbs flashing than tiles, it was surely only a question of time before a plane tried to land on it.

"Adelina, bring the sunglasses."

Oh, no, not Darius again.

"I got a call from Blackpool, they want their illuminations back."

"Don't tease him Darius."

"Good evening Adelina. Darius."

"Good evening, Cedric. Are you all set for Christmas?"

"I think so, Adelina."

"We are just going to the cemetery to visit some relatives. We like to do that on Christmas Eve."

"That's nice."

"Do you have a spade?" asked Darius laughing heartily.

"Ignore him, Cedric. He's had too much eggnog. Come along, Darius."

Cedric watched as they moved down the street, Darius's chortling fading as they disappeared into the darkness. He inserted his key in the lock and opened the door, never mind Darius, he had more important things to think about. The door closed causing Rudolph's nose to glow bright red and the sound of Jingle Bells to fill the air.

Daphne came out of the changing room carrying the police uniform and boots, She looked around the shop, Penelope was nowhere to be seen. Where could she have got to, she thought as she moved down the aisle. She stopped by the fur lined handcuffs and picked them up, examining them closely. She shrugged her shoulders, they might be fun, she added them to her purchases and headed for the cash register.

"Ah, there you are, Penelope. What's in the bag?"

"It's something for you, I think you will like it."

Daphne took the bag.

"You must promise not to open it until Christmas day, Daphy."

"Ok. I thought it might be Cedric's present."

"No, I bought that a few days ago."

"Where have you hidden it this year?"

"Somewhere he will never find it."

I would definitely prefer to do this during the day, thought Cedric as he opened the back door and shone the torch into the darkness. Still, he knew where it was now, it would not take long. He illuminated the birdhouse and walked swiftly across the wet lawn smiling to himself. He shone the beam in through the small opening. It looked empty. No this could not be, Edgar Allen Poe, The Raven. He reached into the hole, the circular wooden edge scrapping along his sleeve as he forced his arm deeper. His fingers stretched until they touched the bottom. They brushed back and forth before retreating in vain. He stood dumbfounded and disheartened, nothing. How could he have gotten it wrong?

Suddenly he brightened up. Penelope said she had seen his golf clubs in the shed a few days ago so obviously she had been inside. What could she possibly have been doing in there other than hiding his present, he reasoned. I have you, Penelope, he smiled with satisfaction as he crossed quickly to the shed. He retracted the bolt and the door swung out. Inside chaos reigned supreme. Around the sides old paint tins were stacked precariously on top of each other intermingled with open sacks of compost. The lawnmower was blocking his entrance. He dragged it out causing the rake and hoe resting against it to crash to the ground. A light went on in the house next door. Cedric instinctively extinguished the torch and remained still. In the window he could see his neighbour looking down, he felt like a burglar in his own garden. The light went out, Cedric heaved a sigh of relief, that's all he needed was another visit from the police after the peeping tom incident. He went into the shed, quietly closing the door and feeling safe put the torch back on. Now where could it be? Behind the paint tins? He started lifting them from the sides for a look. Most were crusted in dry paint, he really should throw them out. They were bought to save money in a wave of DIY optimism that lasted about a week. A half painted bathroom later and with an unimaginable amount splattered on the sink and toilet resulted in Penelope ordering a complete refurbishment and a total false economy.

Nothing behind the paint tins. Cedric scratched his head and looked around. He had it, it must be buried in one of the compost sacks. He placed the torch down and plunged his hands in, ferreting wildly in the damp soil. The smell filled his nostrils as he dug deeper.

Five minutes later his sleeves were covered in dirt and the shed was a bigger mess than before. Worst of all, no present. He exited dejectedly. Where could it be? He put everything back and closed the door before trudging back to the house and into the living room. Daphne's present was still under the tree, Penelope must have forgotten to take it and give it to her today. That was not like her to forget. Thinking of Penelope he realised she would be home soon and he was no nearer to finding it. Another year, another failed quest, he thought plonking down on the sofa and closing his eyes. He had searched everywhere, all the rooms and cupboards, even the one under the stairs, and now the shed and birdhouse. He opened his eyes and stared at the fire place remembering how Sebastain had jibed him about writing a letter to Father Christmas and putting it up the chimney. Beating him at golf today wiped that smug look off his face. That thought cheered Cedric up. That was it, the chimney. Cedric got on his knees and started reaching up it. Soot fell on his face but he did not care, it had to be here, this was going to be his year.

"Cedric, what are you doing down there?"

"Penelope!" he gasped removing his hands and looking around. "I didn't hear you come in."

"Look at the mess you have made," she admonished pointing at the soot covered carpet around him.

"I'll clean it up."

"And what's that dirt on your sleeves?"

"Compost."

"How have you got compost on you? On second thoughts don't tell me, just put your clothes into the washing machine and have a shower before you come to bed."

Cedric traipsed into the kitchen. Penelope watched him pulling his jumper over his head and smiled knowingly.

ACT III

CHRISTMAS DAY

CEDRIC AND PENELOPE'S HOUSE

"Merry Christmas, Cedric," said Penelope sitting up in bed.

She leaned over and kissed him.

"Merry Christmas, Penelope," he replied stretching his arms and legs. "You win again. Where is it?"

"Have you ever read Edgar Allan Poe?"

"No, and I've heard quite enough about Edgar Allen Poe, thank you very much."

"Pity, it would have helped you to find your present?"

"It didn't, I looked."

"Where?"

"I searched the birdhouse last night."

"Ah, The Raven. No, I was thinking of The Purloined Letter."

Cedric looked at her with his brow furrowed.

"Do you want a fried breakfast" she asked getting up and slipping on a dressing gown.

"Lovely, Penelope, then we can open our presents and you can tell me where you hid it."

Penelope went downstairs and Cedric snuggled back under the duvet.

He was awoken by the telephone ringing in the sitting room. Who could that be, he thought. Never mind, Penelope could get it. The ringing continued and continued.

"Penelope!"

No reply but the phone kept ringing.

He got up and went down into the lounge.

"Hello," he said picking up the receiver.

"Merry Christmas, Cedric."

"Daphy? Oh. Yes, merry Christmas."

"I just wanted to thank Penelope for the present."

"What did she get you?"

"Oh, well, something personal."

"Clothes?"

"Um, a type of clothes."

"You're being very mysterious, Daphy."

"I have to go now, just let Penelope know I appreciate the present, I would not have the confidence to buy it myself. Merry Christmas again."

"Who was that, Cedric?"

"Daphy," replied Cedric putting the phone down, "She called to thank you for the present."

"I bought it yesterday for her, I thought she would have fun with it, Sebastian too."

"She was acting very strangely."

"Oh, well, you know Daphy."

"I suppose. Was that a second present you bought for her?"

"No."

"Then whose is that one under the tree?"

Penelope picked up the small gold foil box. She pulled off the name tag "To Daphne" to reveal Cedric's name underneath.

"In The Purloined Letter the stolen document was hidden in plain sight the whole time. Merry Christmas, Cedric."

A HALLOWEEN TALE

"Prices these days, I remember when you could buy a newspaper for thruppence and a loaf of bread for a shilling."

The old man grumbled to himself as he made his way passed the shops along the pavement avoiding the lingering puddles from the earlier morning rain. He pulled his shabby overcoat tightly around his body to keep out the chilling autumn wind. The thick clouds above made it a dark, dismal day. A young woman pushing a pram trundled towards him, she stared at him quizzically, turning her head as she passed. He knew exactly what she was looking at, he had experienced it all his life. His eyes made even more prominent with the spectacles he had been forced to wear in recent years.

More people bustled about around him in both directions, no doubt eager to get home after an arduous day at work. He stopped in front of a shop window decorated with cobwebs and spiders, adjusting his thick lensed spectacles and pressing his face against the glass. Inside a mannequin was dressed in a black cloak and pointed hat, a broomstick in hand and a black cat at its feet. The mask over the face was covered in boils and the nose was long and crooked. Around the walls hung skulls and on the floor pumpkins carved into scary faces.

"Bloody Halloween, I'll be glad when tonight is over."

As he turned and moved away he bumped into a young man wearing a navy suit, the jolt almost knocking his glasses off and pushing him aside so his foot landed in a deep puddle. The old man scowled at him as he felt the water seeping into his old shoes.

"Why don't you look where you're going," he growled after him, adjusting his glasses and watching him disappear among the throng.

"Not even an apology, that sums up the young today, ignorant idlers," he muttered.

He continued along the pavement keen to get out of his wet brogues. As he turned into his street he noticed two young youths sat on the curb outside his house. One was in a grey tracksuit while the other had a white hoodie pulled up over his head obscuring his face. Leaning against his wall behind them was slumped, what seemed to be a drunk man. Drunk at this time of day, it's a disgrace, just look at his nose and lips, all red and swollen and his face all white and pasty. I bet he does not even have a job, thought the old man, who would employ him with that unkempt, wild hair all over the place, just look at the colour of it, purple. As he drew nearer he could see that it was a clown mask. The red mouth was twisted into a distorted grin made more disturbing by the hollow eye sockets. There was a placard propped up on his outstretched legs. He read the sign "POUND FOR THE GUY." He shook his head in disbelief, even the money wanted had increased, everyone knew it was a penny for the guy, not that he had ever given a penny. Come to think of it, he had not seen a guy for years, he supposed it had gone out of fashion like so many things these days. Additionally. Guy Fawkes night was a week away, he had not seen the back of Halloween yet.

"Pound for the guy," said the boy in the hoodie.

From his tone the old man was unsure whether this was a request or a demand. That typified the young these days, entitled wasters.

"Halloween has not gone and you are already collecting for Guy Fawkes night."

"Just a pound," said hoodie.

"It's a penny for the guy, not a pound."

"That's inflation."

"You'll get nothing from me."

"How about those old shoes then?" he said looking derisively at the old man's brogues. "They would look great on our guy."

"I've had these shoes since before you were born, when things were made to last."

"What's wrong with your eyes?" exclaimed the boy in the tracksuit.

"Nothing," replied the old man indignantly.

"One's brown and one's green."

"Never mind about my eyes, just move that guy away from my house, blocking all the pavement like that."

The two youths remained seated grinning insolently.

"I'll get the police on you."

"And tell them what?" sneered hoodie. "There is a guy outside your house?"

"They can arrest him, take him down the cells and beat a confession out of him," added trackie chuckling. "It's getting dark I think we will go but don't worry we'll be around tonight for trick or treat."

"You'll get nothing from me," repeated the old man.

"Then it will be trick. Number 17, isn't it?" said hoodie menacingly.

"Would you like your house decorated with eggs or tomatoes?" added trackie.

No respect, that summed up today's youth, workshy layabouts.

The two youths got up and began to slouch away leaving the guy on the pavement,

"What about this?" called the old man pointing at the prostrate figure.

"Leave it there, we'll be back tomorrow" called hoodie as they lumbered down the street.

The old man made his way up the steps with their laughter ringing in his ears. He opened the door and went inside. The hall was not much warmer than the street. He looked at the clock on the wall, still only half past four, the heating would not come on for another half hour. The price of gas these days, he would just keep his coat on for a while. A hot cup of tea would warm him up.

In the kitchen he opened the cupboard, The crockery was stacked in one neat pile: one plate, one bowl, one cup. He lifted the cup out, filled it almost to the brim with water and poured it into the kettle. While it boiled he opened the drawer below. Inside was one knife, one fork, one table spoon and one tea spoon. He removed the tea spoon and closed the drawer. On the counter above was a plastic tub. He opened it to reveal a single used soggy tea bag. Perfectly good to use a teabag more than once. He put it in the cup trying to remember if this was the second or third time. The water bubbled away through the small window on the side of the kettle. He switched it off, the water would be hot, There was no point wasting money on electricity unnecessarily. He poured the water into the cup and stirred it. The tea was pale yellow. He gave it a vigorous stir which barely changed the colour. Might get one more cup out of the bag, thought the old man scooping it up and dropping it back in the tub. He picked up the cup and went into the lounge. Outside the light was beginning to fade. He looked through the window and could just about make out the guy on the pavement, the wild purple hair just visible above his wall. The bin trucks were due early tomorrow, the men would chuck it in the compactor and it would get crushed and smashed to smithereens, that would teach those two delinquents. It would be torn to shreds while they were still in their beds. He grinned as he walked across the threadbare carpet and slumped down in a sagging, worn armchair, sitting in near darkness. Maybe he could wait another half hour before turning on a lamp. He sipped his tea before settling down and nodding off.

He was awoken by a knock on the door. Who could that be, he wondered, he neither got nor wanted visitors. He ambled up and traipsed down the hall and opened the door. Bloody Halloween, he had forgotten about that as he slumbered peacefully. Outside stood two small children, a boy dressed all in red wearing a set of plastic horns on his head and carrying a long three pronged fork. Beside him was a little girl in a black cloak and pointed hat with a broom stick in her hand.

"Trick or treat," they greeted joyfully in unison holding out small sacks.

"Shouldn't you be at home doing homework," he said grumpily.

"It's Halloween," replied the boy smiling happily.

"That's no excuse to go begging."

"We.re not begging it's trick or treat."

"Ok. Do a trick."

"It doesn't mean a magic trick."

"What does it mean then?"

"You have to give us a treat or we play a trick on you."

"So, it's extortion."

"What's extortion?" asked the small girl.

"If you were at home studying, like you should be, you would know what it meant."

The two children looked at each other perplexed before returning back to the old man.

"Trick or treat," they repeated a little less certainly this time.

A malicious smirk appeared on his face.

"Very well, if you want a treat, I'll give you one. Just wait here."

He closed the door and went into the kitchen. From under the sink he removed a bucket and filled it with water. This would teach the little brats not to pester people. The bucket was almost full to the brim, he moved carefully along the hall so as not to spill any. At the door he concealed it behind his back and opened it. The two children were waiting eagerly with happy faces and sacks open ready. The old man smiled kindly then quickly whipped the bucket in front of him and tossed the water on top of them. For a moment they stood still the smiles on their faces turning to shock, the water dripping off their drenched clothes. Then they burst into tears, turned and ran, dropping their sacks.

"And don't come back," shouted the old man sneering as he listened to their wails fading into the distance.

He bent down and picked up the sacks.

"No point wasting all these sweets," he said looking at the goodies inside and grinning.

He went back inside and closed the door. That was great fun, he thought with relish. He sat down in his armchair and munched on a chocolate bar.

The two bags lay empty on the carpet with candy wrappers strewn around them. The old man reclined back and licked his lips, that was a good scoff, he would not mind a bit more, this trick or treat lark was not all bad, he reflected. His eyes lit up as he heard the rap on his front door. He got up and crept to the window, peeling back the curtain slightly until he could see through the narrow crack. A group of four youngsters were waiting expectantly, one holding a bulging sack. Yummy, thought the old man. He went into the hall and took a long handled brush from the cupboard under the stairs. He tiptoed to the front door, a malevolent grin spreading across his craggy face. This was going to be fun. He stopped and listened to the children giggling outside. There was another knock on the door, he waited patiently, his hand inching towards the handle.

"There's no-one in."

"Knock again, Jonny."

The old man put his hand on the doorknob and tightened his grip on the brush handle, pointing it threateningly forward.

"Go on, Jonny."

As the knock resounded on the wood the old man hurled the door open, the young boy's hand frozen in midair ready to knock. He looked at the brush pointing menacingly at him.

"Trick or treat," he said quietly with a mixture of puzzlement and uncertainty.

"Treat!" shouted the old man. "And here it is."

With that he thrust the brush into the boy's chest causing him to stumble backwards and drop the bag.

"Run!" he yelled as he turned and fled past the other boys.

The boys followed hastily, the old man giving chase, getting within range of the smallest boy and pushing him violently in the back. He fell face first into one of the puddles still remaining after the morning rain. The murky water splashed into his face and soaked into his batman costume, the cloak sinking into the pool. He staggered to his feet and ran away sobbing, the old man's cruel laughter ringing in his ears. He picked up the bag, went back inside, closed the door and locked it. That was enough fun for one night. He sat back down in his armchair to revel in his bounty.

He was awoken by a hammering at the door. Three loud knocks that were loud enough to wake the dead. Who the hell is that, he thought grumpily, looking at the clock on the mantlepiece with bleary eyes. Midnight. Who was at his door at midnight? Whoever it was they could stay there, he was not getting up to answer it. The whole house resounded as the front door was pounded three more times even louder than the first, enough to make the old man jump.

"Bloody kids. I'll teach them to knock on my door at this ungodly hour," he grumbled as he put his hands on the armrests and pushed himself to his feet.

He ambled across the room, out into the hall and got his brush from under the stairs. The door shook as it boomed to three more knocks. The old man gritted his teeth as he scowled and tightened his grip on the long wooden handle. He opened the door. In the darkness stood a tall, slender figure in a black, hooded robe. The wide sleeves covered his hands and the bottom trailed along the ground concealing his feet. He was tall, surely over seven feet tall. The old man craned his neck up but the hood completely hid his face and he found himself looking into a black hole. The sight made him shudder and weaken his grip on the brush so it drooped from his limp hands.

"Trick or treat."

The figure spoke slowly with a soft voice made eerily sinister by his appearance. The old man composed himself.

"You're a bit old for trick or treat."

"One is never to old, I always make my visits on Halloween."

"Well, I have nothing for you," growled the old man regaining his resolve.

"Then let it be trick."

The figure spoke the words deliberately and menacingly.

They stood silently before each other. An icy wind seemed to cut through the old man to his very soul. He shivered but steeled himself, his eyes hardening and narrowing as he viewed the figure stood perfectly still.

"Go to the devil," raged the old man.

He slammed the door shut ramming the bolt closed and inserting the chain. Back in the living room he peeled a curtain back and peered through the crack. The figure was gone.

He traipsed to the cabinet and poured himself a brandy. Holding it in both hands he lifted it to his lips and swallowed the whole lot in one gulp. He sighed deeply as he put the glass down going back to the curtain and looking through the crack into the darkness. In the street all was quiet and still.

"Bloody Halloween," he muttered closing the curtain.

He ambled up the stairs to his bedroom, put on his nightgown and got between the sheets. Tomorrow Halloween would be over. He switched off his bedside lamp, closed his eyes and drifted off to sleep.

However, he did not sleep peacefully, his mind was tormented by visions, the constant knocking at his door growing louder and louder. In the bed he tossed and turned, the sheets being scattered and falling to the floor. In his mind the door was flung open with a crash and heavy footsteps stomped down the hall until they reached the stairs. The whole house shook as the footsteps pounded on the stairs, increasing in volume as they got nearer and nearer to the top. He thrashed around the bed and began to groan in anguish. The door knob turned slowly, until it opened gradually inch by inch. His groans turned to wails as the figure glided towards him, elevating from the ground and floating above him. The old man gasped and eyes bulged open. He breathed rapidly as he stared through wild eyes into the darkness. It was just a bad dream, he let out a sigh of relief. He reached across to the bedside table and turned on the lamp. The room became dimly lit. He squinted at the clock. The hands were aligned on the twelve. Midnight. How could that be? Had the clock stopped? He picked it up and held it to his ear. Tick, tock, tick, tock. He put it down and looked at the hands, they were frozen at midnight. Suddenly, he felt an icy gust across his face and looked towards the foot of the bed and the shadowy robed figure standing motionless. He scrambled frantically for his glasses on the table, putting them on and looking down the bed. The room was empty. He was startled by the sudden banging of a door downstairs. With trepidation he arose and made his way out onto the landing, putting his hand on the light switch and pressing. The landing remained dark. He toggled the switch up and down but nothing.

"Who's there?" he called in the darkness.

No reply.

"I know someone's there."

The door slammed even more ferociously. Apprehensively he descended, cautiously feeling each step. The door slammed again sending a shiver down his spine. At the bottom he pressed the hall light switch, that was not working either. He felt the cold air rushing from the front door and made his way gingerly to it. The door was wide open and the wind banging it against the inside wall causing a dent and the paint to flake to the ground. How could this be, he was certain he had bolted and chained it? He shut it, slid the bolt across firmly and attached the chain. As he retreated down the pitch black hall perplexed and disturbed he became aware of a creaking coming from the living room. He stopped abruptly and listened. Someone was pacing slowly across the floorboards. He crept silently to the cupboard under the stairs and quietly eased open the door. Inside he ferreted around until his hand closed around a thick wooden handle, He lifted the heavy object and ran his hand along the cold steel blade. He held the axe aloft and moved to the living room door. Inside the pacing had ceased and it was quiet. He put his hand onto the knob and opened it. A small lamp was dimly illuminating the room. He entered slowly, the axe above his head ready to strike.

"Come in, I've been waiting for you," said the soft voice he had heard before.

In his chair sat the hooded figure, his arms along the rests, his hands covered by the sleeves of the robe which hung down over the edge of the chair while the bottom of the robe was spread along the floor obscuring his feet.

"What do you want?" said the old man putting both hands on the axe and lifting it higher so the blade was dipped behind his back. "I am not afraid to use this."

The figure was silent and motionless.

"I will," continued the old man threateningly but his trembling voice unable to mask his fear. "The law will protect me, you have broken in."

The figure said nothing.

"If you don't leave I'll do it."

He tightened his grip on the axe.

"What good is an axe without a blade?" said the figure calmly.

Behind the old man resounded a metallic clank as the blade slipped from the handle and hit the floor. He spun around and looked at it with increasing panic.

"Let's talk about you," said the figure with icy tranquillity. "You have failed to live a good life and must be taught a lesson."

"What are you going to do. Send three ghosts?"

"No. Only one."

The menace in his voice made the old man's whole body tremble.

"You can't frighten me," he croaked with a shaking voice. "I'm calling the police."

He went to the sideboard and picked up the phone punching in the numbers 9-9-9.

"What good is a phone if you cannot speak?" said the figure.

"Hello, emergency service operator, which service do you require?"

The old man opened his mouth to speak but made no sound.

"Which service, please? Fire, police or ambulance?"

Again he tried to speak but was unbale to form the words. He felt a cold, bony hand remove the receiver from his.

"Sorry, I rang in error," said the figure replacing the phone.

The old man stumbled back against the wall, his eyes wild with terror. He staggered from the room and out into the hallway, stumbling to the front door as the figure followed serenely. He scrambled to undo the chain, constantly glancing over his shoulder at the approaching figure. His fingers closed around the bolt, yanking it open and flinging open the door. He looked out into the street, stepped forward and fell flat on his face. He lay prostrate, unable to move, his whole body seemed paralysed.

"And now we have reached the end," spoke the figure peacefully.

173

He felt the cold, bony hands close around his ankles.

Dawn was breaking as the bin truck trundled along the street and stopped outside the old man's house. The front door was shut and all the curtains closed. On the pavement the guy was slumped against the wall, the head drooped so the face was buried on the chest and the wild purple hair all around. The men dismounted from the truck and began emptying the bins into the disposer at the rear.

"What about the guy?" asked the younger worker.

"Better chuck it in." replied his older colleague.

The young man bent down and lofted it over his shoulder so the head and arms hung limply down his back.

"Bloody hell, it's heavy," he said carrying it to the disposer.

"Toss it in and turn it on."

He tipped the guy backwards onto the rest of the rubbish so it landed face up before moving to the side of the vehicle and pressing the button. The huge metal teeth of the grinder began to descend towards the guy. Through the holes in the clown mask two eyes darted wildly, one brown and one green.

CEDRIC AND THE

FORTUNE TELLER

Characters

Cedric, thirtysomething socialite

Penelope, Cedric's wife

Daphne, friend of Cedric & Penelope

Sebastian, Daphne's husband

Madame Astrea, the fortune teller

Esmeralda, mystic shop assistant

ACT I

SCENE 1

FRIDAY

CEDRIC AND PENELOPE'S HOUSE

Cuckoooo! Cuckoooo!

The small wooden bird appeared from the clock hanging in the landing.

"Hurry up, Cedric, that's ten o'clock, the taxi will be here soon."

"I'll just get the skis out of the loft."

"You should have just left them in the hall with the suitcases and the boots."

"They were blocking the way."

"Well, get them now. I'm going to phone Daphne to let her know we will meet them at the airport" said Penelope descending the stairs.

Cedric picked up the vanity chair from the bedroom and placed it on the landing below the loft. He stood on it and pushed open the hatch . He put his hands in and ferreted about until he could feel the ski bag. It was heavy but he managed to drag it until it appeared in the gap above. Gently he tilted it and lowered it down.

"I told you before you should use the step ladder, that chair will not support your weight," admonished Penelope reappearing.

"It's perfectly fine, Penelope," replied Cedric closing the hatch and stepping down.

"Look at the foot imprints! You have crushed all the velvet!"

"That's easily fixed," said Cedric fluffing the velvet up with his hands, "See, as good as new."

BEEP! BEEP!"

"That's the taxi now, Cedric, let's go."

They descended the stairs, picked up the luggage and opened the front door.

"Good morning Penelope, good morning Cedric."

Oh, no, Darius.

"Good morning Darius, good morning Adelina," replied Penelope opening the taxi door.

"You go for your holiday today, yes?" said Adelina in her thick Romanian accent.

"That's right, three wonderful days in St. Moritz."

"I hope you are having a nice time."

"Thank you, Adelina.

"Cedric, make sure the yeti does not get you," shouted Darius chuckling.

Cedric got into the car quickly and closed the door. Every time he saw Darius he had some fresh jibe for him and all because he thought he was a vampire when he moved into the street. It had got so bad he would peek through the window to check he was not about before leaving the house. At least he would have three glorious days Darius free.

Penelope checked her phone.

"I just got a text from Daphne, she is already at the airport with Sebastian.

Cedric's joy was short lived. Three days with Sebastian.

SCENE 2

AT THE AIRPORT

"These goggles are the latest in cutting edge technology and fashion, Oakley Flight Deck. Guess how much, Cedric?

"I've no idea Sebastian."

No good morning, no hello, just straight to how much, and I've got to endure this for the whole weekend, thought Cedric.

"The lens is 100% Prizm iridium."

Cedric looked at the goggles perched on top of his head, the light reflecting off the mirrored tint.

"Go on, guess how much?"

"£80."

"Higher."

£100."

"Higher."

"I give up," said Cedric wearily.

"£200."

Cedric prayed to God the flight was on time and their seats were apart. Hopefully, Sebastian's would be at the back near the luggage hold, or preferably, in it.

"The flight is delayed," said Daphne.

Thanks a lot, thought Cedric looking upwards.

"Never mind, we can get a drink while we wait," said Penelope. "I like your ski jacket, Daphy,"

Daphne was wearing a bright red jacket with a fur lined collar.

"It's new, I only bought it last week in Harrods, the fur is lovely and warm."

"It looks it."

"As we are delayed I think I'll pop into that shop over there."

"The Mystic Witch," said Cedric looking at the small shop with a black pentagram painted on the glass front. "What kind of a shop is that?"

"It probably has things for spirituality and wellness."

"It looks like it sells things for summoning the devil."

"No. it's not like that at all. Although there might be some amulets for keeping evil spirits away. Who wants to come in with me?"

Penelope, Cedric and Sebastian started walking in the opposite direction towards the bar.

"I can tell you about my new skis, Cedric," said Sebastian. "You'll never guess how much?"

"I'll come with you, Daphy."

The shop was softly lit with the light aroma of incense burning and slow melodic piano music playing over the sound of a gently running stream. The ambience immediately melting away all Cedric's thoughts of Sebastian and Darius. He looked at the chalices, candle holders and globes on the shelves and the statues on the table in the centre. He picked up a bronze statue of an angel. The winged arms were lifted and it was holding a six pointed star above its head.

"That's Metaron," said Daphne.

"Metatron?"

"Yes, it is the name that Enoch received when he transformed into an angel."

"How do you know that, Daphy?"

"I take a great interest in mysticism and spirituality. I would love to go to Stonehenge for the Summer Solstice. Sebastian never wants to go, perhaps we could go together?"

"Hmm," mumbled Cedric turning the statue and looking underneath the base."

"£65!"

"That is a wonderful piece, hand painted," said the woman behind the counter. "It is an Archangel of immense spirituality and wisdom. It will guide and support you in your life. I am Esmeralda, let me know if you require any assistance.

Cedric looked at her flowing white dress with wide sleeves hanging over her forearms exposing the multiple coloured bangles on each wrist which jangled as she gestured towards the statue. Around her neck hung several necklaces of different sized beads and her jet black hair cascaded wildly around her shoulders down to her waist.

"I love shops like this," gushed Daphne. "I wonder what it was before this."

"Certainly not a hairdressers," mumbled Cedric.

"Oh, just look at this beautiful candle holder, Cedric, decorated with the seven Chakras that bring peace. Don't you think this would look wonderful on the mantlepiece?"

"I guess," replied Cedric unconvinced.

He moved around the table looking at all the cauldrons and wands fully expecting Harry Potter to appear at any moment.

"Oh, Cedric, look at this."

She was pointing at a beaded curtain draped over a doorway to the floor. Through the beads Cedric could see a light flickering in the dim room behind. Above the frame in gothic lettering were the words, Madame Astrea, Fortune Teller."

"Let's go in, Cedric."

"You don't believe in this nonsense, do you Daphy?" said Cedric a little too loudly causing Esmeralda to look at him sternly.

"You don't believe in this nonsense?" he repeated in a whisper.

"It's not nonsense, a psychic told me I was going to marry Sebastian."

"You could probably sue her."

"What?"

"Nothing."

"She did not actually say Sebastian but she said a rich and handsome man."

And big-headed, thought Cedric.

"Considering you only mix in society circles that is hardly an earth shattering revelation."

"I did not tell her my background."

"You did not need to, as soon as you spoke she knew, Daphy."

"What's wrong with the way I speak?"

"Nothing, but it's not exactly what you would find in an East End market."

"Come on," said Daphne peeling back the curtain beads and going in followed by a reluctant Cedric.

Inside an old woman sat behind a circular table, dimly illuminated by the candles surrounding the room. A black lace shawl covered her head and was wrapped around her shoulders. In front of her stood a white opaque crystal ball upon which she gently placed her fingers.

"Welcome, I am Madame Astrea, I have been expecting you, Daphy," said the old woman in a dreamy voice that seemed to float on the air.

"See she knows my nickname, Cedric."

"Probably heard me say it outside the door," murmured Cedric.

"Please, sit, you too Cedric."

"She knows your name too!."

"You just said it."

"First cross my palm with silver."

"Is Visa ok?" said Daphne removing the card from her bag.

"Perfect," replied Madame Astrea producing a card reader from under the table.

Daphne tapped the card on top.

"These fortune tellers have certainly embraced modern technology," muttered Cedric.

"Let us begin," said Madame Astrea placing her long bony fingers back on the crystal ball and staring intensely into it.

Cedric watched as she gently caressed the sphere, her fingers adorned with rings of different coloured gemstones.

"I see you going on a journey."

How does she do it? It's a miracle. I suppose that we are in the middle of Heathrow airport is a bit of a clue.

"I see the colour white."

Now in fairness that could just be the actual crystal ball she's seeing.

"Snow, I see snow."

"That's amazing! Yes, I am going skiing in St. Moritz," gushed Daphne excitedly.

I wonder if the fact that Daphne is wearing a skiing jacket helped at all.

"I see you having a happy time with much fun and relaxation."

Who would have thought a skiing holiday would involve fun and relaxation?

"That's wonderful news. Can you see anything about my husband?"

"Sebastian? Let me look," she replied staring earnestly in the globe.

How did she know Daphy's husband's name was Sebastian? Neither of them had said it either in here or in the shop.

Suddenly his thoughts were interrupted by the airport public address system.

"Would all passengers travelling to Zurich on flight BA6734 please proceed immediately to gate 12."

"That's our flight, Daphy, they must have brought the take-off time forward," said Cedric getting up.

"Aw, that's a shame. Thank you anyway Madame Astrea."

They walked towards the beaded door.

"WAIT!" screamed Madame Astrea.

They looked back in surprise at the fortune teller gripping the crystal ball tight and staring deeply within with a concerned look etched on her face.

"I see an accident."

"An accident? That's terrible," exclaimed Daphne.

"Yes, there is no doubt, you are going to break a leg."

"Oh, no," swooned Daphne.

"No, not you. You," she pronounced stretching out her arm and pointing her bony finger at Cedric." "Before midnight on Sunday you will break a leg."

Back in the shop Cedric stood in a daze. It had to be nonsense it just had to be. How can you see the future in a crystal ball, it was impossible. And yet she had known Sebastian's name and that was impossible too. That was it, the dice had been cast, he was going to break a leg, probably in some horrific accident.

"That's it, I'm not going skiing. If I go home and stay in bed until midnight Sunday I can avoid breaking a leg."

"You need something to fight off the evil spirits," said Esmeralda listening. "I can recommend this."

"A voodoo doll?"

Cedric looked incredulously at the small material doll dressed in a black robe and white sash. Wild black hair shot out in all directions from the head, in fact, not unlike Esmeralda's, he thought.

"It's not a voodoo doll, it's a wanga doll."

"What's the difference?"

"A voodoo doll is used to target someone else, maybe an enemy you want to harm, whereas a wanga doll is directed at the user. This one is for protection."

"No, thank you," declined Cedric politely, contemplating that a voodoo doll to use on Sebastian was not without appeal. He was severely tempted to ask if she had any that could make someone mute.

"This wanga doll is capable of summoning supernatural forces of the night to work on behalf of the person who possesses it. Only £40."

I knew it, thought Cedric, it's a scam. The fortune teller tells of some impending tragedy so they can make a sale in the shop. His worries began to recede.

"You need something to ward off the portent," pressured Daphne.

"I'm sure I'll be fine," said Cedric feeling more relaxed and moving towards the door.

"What about Madame Astrea's warning?"

"It's all made up," he whispered ensuring Esmeralda could not overhear.

"She knew our names."

"Probably heard us talking in the shop. I wouldn't be surprised if there is a microphone and camera connected to her room," said Cedric scanning the shop for them.

"She knew Sebastian's name. I didn't say it and I can't remember you saying it either."

Cedric paused, his anxiety returning rapidly as he remembered that. His face began to go pale.

"I'll buy you the doll," offered Daphne.

"I'll look stupid carrying a doll."

"We have amulets," called Esmeralda.

"Excellent," enthused Daphne returning it the counter with Cedric traipsing reluctantly behind.

Esmeralda moved over to a wall display full of amulets hanging from necklaces. Cedric looked unconvincingly at the amulets of cats, crickets and ladybugs. How was a ladybug going to protect him, he thought sceptically.

"How about this one," suggested Daphne picking up a silver oval amulet with a large blue eye in the middle.

"The Eye of Horus," said Esmeralda. "It is one of the most powerful protectors against misfortune. This one has been purified and consecrated."

"I'm not wearing that" said Cedric looking disconcertedly at the eye staring up at him and wondering what purified and consecrated meant.

"How about a pentacle or witch's knot?" proposed Daphne.

Cedric looked at the occult symbols wondering if in fact he would not prefer to have a broken leg.

"Or a horn?"

Daphne took it down and handed it to him.

This was actually quite ornate, he thought, studying the small red horn with a silver crown on top. He could probably wear this without looking like he was going to a black mass.

"The horn originated in southern Italy where it is known as the cornicello," informed Esmeralda. "When malevolence is near you turn the horn with your fingers until the evil has passed."

Cedric put it around his neck and twisted it in his fingers.

"That really suits you, Cedric," complimented Daphne.

"Ok. I'll take the horn,"

"That will be £50."

"£50!"

"This is an authentic cornicello from Naples "said Esmeralda.

"Better than having a broken leg," added Daphne.

Cedric took out his wallet.

They left the shop and approached Penelope and Sebastian. They both stared at the amulet around Cedric's neck.

What is it this time, thought Penelope sighing resignedly.

"Have you joined the Moonies, Cedric?" asked Sebastian.

"No, Sebastian, I have not joined the Moonies."

"Then why are you wearing what appears to be a chilli around your neck?"

"It's not a chilli, it's a cornicello."

"A what?"

"A cornicello."

"It's to protect him from evil spirits," said Daphne supportively.

"My mistake, you have not joined the Moonies, you've joined the Golden Dawn."

"We had better go to the gate," said Cedric heading speedily across the concourse. Behind him he could hear Daphne relaying the story of the fortune teller to Sebastian and Penelope.

"Cabin doors closed for take-off."

Cedric looked out through the window, Penelope beside him and Sebastian and Daphne across the aisle.

"Well, you managed to get up the stairs to the plane without breaking your leg, so far so good," said Sebastian.

"That's it I'm not going."

"They have closed the doors," said Penelope.

"Well, I'm not skiing then."

"You're being silly Cedric, you love skiing. Anyway, I thought you did not believe in fortune tellers."

"I don't, or at least, I didn't."

"Well then. It was easy for her to know you were going on a skiing holiday and your names."

"What about knowing Sebastian's name?"

"You or Daphy must have said it at some point."

"I cannot recall doing so, neither can Daphy."

"Well, she probably tells everyone going on a skiing holiday they are going to break a leg. There's always one or two on the return flight with their leg in a cast so she's bound to be right sometimes."

Cedric fell silent occupied by his thoughts, he only had to get safely to midnight Sunday. He sat quietly, turning the horn in his fingers.

ACT II

SCENE 1

SATURDAY

ST. MORITZ

"What a wonderful day," said Penelope looking up at the clear blue sky and feeling the sun warm her cheeks below her goggles.

"And what a spectacular view," added Daphne looking at the snow covered peaks around them.

"Good skiing conditions," said Sebastian shuffling his skis back and forth in the soft snow and prodding it with his pole. "Lovely and smooth.

Cedric looked apprehensively down the slope feeling the horn below his ski suit.

"Perhaps we should start on an easy run."

"What! No, we want to get on those blacks, the Hahnansee run down to St. Moritz Bad and the glacier run from Diazolezza to Morteratsch."

"Oh, yes, it's beautiful skiing down through the pine trees," gushed Daphne.

"I heard it's best to get a guide for the glacier run," said Cedric concerned.

"I have done it lots of times," boasted Sebastian. "I'm better than a guide."

"You said you were looking forward to doing the glacier run, Cedric," said Penelope.

"That was before."

"Before what?"

"You know."

"Oh, no, surely you're not still dwelling on that fortune teller?"

"I think I'll get a coffee."

"We've only just got on the slopes," said Sebastian testily. "The best snow is always in the morning before the sun softens it and it has been skied over repeatedly."

"This is an easy run to start," said Penelope encouragingly.

"Let's go," instructed Sebastian decisively, lowering his goggles over his eyes and pushing off with his sticks. "See you at the bottom."

"You'll be fine," said Daphne. "Do you have your horn?"

"It's under my jacket."

"Well then, that will keep you safe."

Cedric watched as Penelope and Daphne followed Sebastian down the slope. He pressed his hand against his chest feeling the horn again. He bit his lip and shuffled slowly forward, easing his way down. He traversed to the right before turning gently and heading across to the left. Skiers whizzed past him as he zigzagged his way to the bottom where the others were waiting.

"You're not going to ski like that all day are you?" complained Sebastain.

"Cedric is a very good skier," said Daphne supportively. "It's alright for you Sebastian you haven't been told by a fortune teller that you are going to break a leg."

"A fortune teller in an airport lobby."

"What's wrong with that?"

"It doesn't sound very psychic to me. Do you think the Oracle of Delphi had a stall at the port of Piraeus or Nostradamus hung about Marseille harbour?"

"You are so cynical, Sebastian. The world is more mystical than we know."

"You're not going to go on about voodoo again are you Daphne, we're here to ski. The glacier is this way."

Sebastian skied towards the chair lift.

"Don't take any notice of him Cedric," said Daphne.

Cedric wished he had bought a voodoo doll that looked something like Sebastian.

Cedric looked out from the top of the glacier, it was as spectacular as he had envisaged, the long sweeping white slope surrounded by tall pine trees illuminated by the radiant sun shining in the clear blue sky. He felt the gentle breeze chill his exposed cheeks. The memory of the fortune teller rescinded as he glided serenely down the slope. The skis ran smoothly beneath his feet as though they were part of his body. He swept past Penelope and Daphne as he gathered speed, feeling the exhilaration as the skis carved the snow. Up ahead was Sebastian. He drew nearer and nearer until he was skiing directly behind him. Sebastian glanced over his shoulder, steeled himself and went into a tuck as he pointed the skis straight down the slope and accelerated. Cedric followed suit and the two of them raced downwards, the skids whooshing across the snow. In the middle of the slope stood a long line of trees, the run splitting to the right and left. Sebastain turned to the right, This is my chance to get ahead, thought Cedric as he cut to the left. They could see each other sporadically between the gaps in the trees. Cedric was nudging ahead, the cafe was at the bottom. Sebastain had no intention of letting Cedric get there first. He tucked as low as he could to get more speed. The skies raced across the snow. He looked sideways through the trees, he was in the lead and the cafe was just ahead. He was going to win, a smile spread across his face. That was the last thing he thought as he tumbled into the snow and rolled down the hill coming to a crumpled heap just in front of the cafe.

"Are you alright Sebastian?" asked Cedric.

Sebastain sat up groggily, covered in snow. He spluttered and spat out a mouthful. One of his skis had become detached in the fall and was wedged under a table.

"The right is the harder side," he gasped trying to regain his breath.

"They looked the same to me," replied Cedric suppressing a grin.

"No, no, there's a big difference, Ask anyone here."

The waiter approached carrying the escaped ski.

"You are lucky the snow is soft today, you might have broken a leg," he said. "You should always come down the easier side if you are inexperienced."

This was getting better by the minute thought Cedric.

"Next time come down the right."

Cedric's day was complete.

"Oh, Sebastian, are you ok?" gushed Daphne arriving at the restaurant with Penelope.

She quickly sprang out of her skis and ran to him, kneeling down and brushing the snow from his jacket.

"I'm perfectly alright, don't fuss so, Daphne."

"What happened?" asked Penelope.

"Sebastian fell," said Cedric fighting to suppress his gleeful laughter.

"Just a slight tumble," defended Sebastain.

"Ploughed his face right into the snow," said Cedric wondering if anyone had captured it on their phone.

"There must have been a bare patch,"

"You should always come down the right," advised Penelope.

Cedric almost wet himself.

SCENE 2

SUNDAY MORNING

CEDRIC AND PENELOPE'S HOTEL ROOM

So far, so good, Cedric had got through Saturday without breaking a leg. Either the fortune teller was a fraud, which he was certain was the case, or the horn was doing its job. He decided to keep it around his neck just in case, He had been skiing well yesterday and he only had to get through until this evening when they left for the airport. They should be back home by midnight and the fortune teller would be proved wrong. He wondered if he was entitled to his money back.

"Sebastian wants to go on the Cresta bobsleigh run this morning," said Penelope putting down the room phone.

"We are not going to ski today?"

"Sebastain isn't keen, according to Daphy.

That did not surprise Cedric, he had been so unnerved by his spectacular fall he had spent the rest of yesterday skiing at the back behind Daphne.

"We are booked in for ten o'clock."

That suited Cedric, it would avoid any potential leg breaks skiing. Unless the bobsleigh crashed. What if the bobsleigh crashed, he thought worriedly. They go around the track at one hell of a pace. He had read somewhere that the bobsleigh can reach up to 93 miles per hour. And they go right up the embankments until they are almost vertical. Suppose it flew out over the top of the track? That's how he was going to break a leg, crashing in a bobsleigh at 93 miles per hour.

"I'm not going."

"You have been wanting to do the Cresta bobsleigh run for ages, Cedric."

"I've changed my mind, it's too dangerous."

"Too dangerous? You were skiing yesterday like you were Franz Klammer on his gold medal winning run at Innsbruck."

"Well, I don't want to tempt fate."

"Are you still preoccupied with what the fortune teller told you?"

"No," he said twisting the horn. "Those bobsleighs can get up to 93 miles per hour."

"Maybe an Olympic team can go at 93 miles per hour but this is for holiday makers, it will not be going anywhere near as fast as that."

"I suppose so," said Cedric unconvinced.

"Anyway Daphne and Sebastian will be waiting so we had better go. I'm sure you'll really enjoy it when we get there."

SCENE 3

THE CRESTA RUN

Cedric looked down the track with increasing trepidation, it certainly seemed steeper than on the television. He watched as a bobsleigh shot around a curve below,. Faster too, he thought.

"Perhaps we can do it another time. Penelope"

"We are going home this evening, plus it is all paid for."

"What's the matter Cedric? Are you getting cold feet," said Sebastian gleefully.

"No, I just don't think it's the right conditions, that's all."

"Rubbish, the instructor told me this is the best it has been all year. I'm sure you can steer it just fine."

"I've got to drive it!" said Cedric horrified. "I thought there was a qualified driver."

"I told them you could drive because you are such a brilliant skier."

Cedric went white.

"Don't tease him, Sebastian," rebuked Daphne. "Of course, there is a driver and a brakeman. We just sit in the middle, it's all very easy."

Bloody Sebastian, perhaps his bobsleigh would fly off the course, that would wipe the smug grin off his face.

"I am Hans, I will be driving the bobsleigh," said a tall athletic man approaching them in a skin tight racing suit that outlined his muscular body. "And this is Karl, he will sit at the back and work the brake."

Cedric looked at Karl, he was a huge man with even more pronounced muscles than Hans' wondering if he was related to Arnold Schwarzenegger at all.

"The first two can get in," advised Hans.

Sebastian made his way along the mat to the bobsleigh.

"Hold on Sebastian," said Daphne. "My helmet is too loose, I think I need a smaller one."

"They are waiting for us, Daphne."

"I need to change it, let Cedric and Penelope go first."

Sebastian reluctantly stepped off the mat muttering grumpily.

"You had better go first."

Cedric surveyed at the sleek bobsleigh, the black metal gleaming under the radiant sun, it looked fast, very fast.

"Better get in then, Cedric," said Penelope moving along the mat.

Cedric twiddled his horn and followed.

"Sit in the middle." directed Hans.

Penelope lowered herself in and Cedric slipped in behind. It was low, very low, he could only just see over the side.

"We will push the bobsleigh off and then jump in, remember to lean when we go into the bends," said Hans. "Ready Karl?"

Karl positioned himself at the rear of the bobsleigh, nodded and lowered his visor. He pulled out the side bar and gripped it with both hands.

"One last thing," added Hans moving to the front and lowering the sidebar, "at the bottom there is no mat so be careful getting out, it is very slippy."

He turned and faced forward, gripping the bar and lowering his body into an almost sprint position.

Cedric's heart was beating through his chest.

The bobsleigh starting rocking back and forth.

Hans gave the command.

"Eins, zwei, drei, vier!"

The bobsleigh moved along the track, Cedric listened to the blades cutting through the ice and the accompanying foot pounding as the two men pushed the sleigh faster and breaking into a run. The sleigh accelerated, suddenly the two men leapt into the sleigh, Cedric felt Karl's legs spread around him as he tucked in behind. The sleigh got faster and faster. Cedric felt the wind rushing against his exposed cheeks. The sleigh tilted as they went into the first bend, leaning more and more as it climbed the curve before speeding onto a straight section. The whole sleigh vibrated as it sped across the hard ice. It raced under a covered section, tilting right and left as it entered a series of bends, rising so much as to be almost vertical. The horn bounced around Cedric's chest.

Finally the sleigh slowed and came to rest, Cedric was panting with the sheer exhilaration. Hans and Karl lifted themselves out.

"You get out first, Penelope," said Cedric whose legs were trapped by her body.

"Let me help," offered Hans taking her hand and assisting her up.

Cedric gripped the sides and lifted himself up, stepping on to the ice.

"That was great," he enthused walking towards Penelope. "Aaaaargh."

His foot shot from underneath him, his body rising before plummeting towards the hard ice below. The horn hit him in the face, this was it, the fruition of the fortune teller's prediction. He felt a big hand grab the front of his jacket and yank him roughly upright before he hit the ground.

"It is very slippy, yes," said Karl releasing him. "You could have broken a leg."

"Danke, Karl," thanked Penelope. "You never listen, Cedric."

The next bobsleigh pulled in behind them and Daphne and Sebastain got out.

"That was wonderful, "gushed Daphne.

"Cedric almost fell, "said Penelope.

"Your horn is keeping you safe."

"You don't need protection from a mystical horn," derided Sebastian walking towards Cedric, "That's just foolishne-aaaaargh."

WHACK!

He hit the ground with a thump.

Cedric looked at his prostrate body on the ice. It would look bad if he burst out laughing, he pinched his arm.

"Oh, Sebastian, are you alright," shrieked Daphne.

Hans knelt down and checked him.

"You are lucky, nothing broken," he said helping him to his feet.

Sebastian was gripping his right buttock.

As he turned Cedric could see the seat of his trousers was torn exposing his underpants and what was that printed on them, yes, it was superman.

Cedric pinched his arm harder.

(Back in the hotel room)

"We are just packing now. We'll meet you in reception," said Penelope putting down the phone.

"Daphne says Sebastian has a massive bruise on his bum. It's not funny," she admonished as Cedric rolled around the bed in paroxysms of laughter.

"She had to put ice on it."

Cedric buried his face in the pillow while his entire body shuddered with mirth.

"You are so immature, Cedric."

It was dark when the plane landed back in England.

"See, it was wise to buy the horn," said Daphne. "It kept you safe Cedric,"

"I suppose so, Daphy."

"We'll see you next week."

Cedric watched as Sebastian walked away limping, He stifled his chuckling under the stern gaze of Penelope.

"Don't start that again, Cedric. Come on let's get a taxi."

What a great holiday.

ACT III

SCENE 1

SUNDAY NIGHT

BACK HOME

The taxi drove away as Cedric and Penelope ambled wearily along the path in the darkness to the front door dragging their luggage behind them.

"Oooo, it's chilly, Penelope."

"The heating should be on, I set it before we left."

They went inside and Cedric dropped the skis in the hall.

"Don't just leave them there, Cedric. Put them back in the loft."

"Can't it wait until tomorrow? It's almost midnight."

"No, just do it now. I don't like them cluttering the place up. You do that while I put the clothes into the washing machine."

Cedric traipsed sluggishly up the stairs dragging the skis behind.

"And use the step ladder," called Penelope from below as he disappeared along the landing.

"Where is it?"

"In the shed, where it always is."

He glanced up at the cuckoo clock, one minute to midnight, the fortune teller had been wrong. It was just as he suspected, these clairvoyants were all charlatans. He went into the bedroom and took off his coat, looking at the horn hanging around his neck. What a lot of nonsense, he thought, slipping it off and placing it on the dressing table. He looked through the window at the frost on the ground. I'm not going out again in that, he decided. He picked up the vanity chair and went back onto the landing. Downstairs he could hear Penelope bustling about in the kitchen, it would only take him a minute, she would never know. He stood on the chair and opened the loft hatch.

CRASH!

Penelope raced up the stairs to discover Cedric laying in a crumpled heap on the floor clutching his leg with an anguished look on his face.

"I've broken it, Penelope, the fortune teller was right, the prophecy has come true."

"Let me see," said Penelope crouching down and raising his trouser leg. "It looks alright to me, it would be swollen if it was broken."

"But the fortune teller?"

"You would be in agony if it was broken. You don't seem to be in agony."

Cedric looked down apprehensively at his exposed leg. It did indeed seem alright. He moved his foot gingerly from right to left, it felt alright.

Cuckoooo! Cuckoooo!

"Midnight, Penelope, the fortune teller's prediction was wrong."

"No, she was right. I told you not to stand on the vanity chair, you have broken one of the legs."

A J BOOTHMAN

OTHER BOOKS

TWIST IN THE TALE VOLUME 1

The Attic, Sheeba, Vampire, A Dark Winter's Tale, Swipe Right, Stranger in The Night, Snake, Ice, The Last Train, Trench Warfare

TWIST IN THE TALE VOLUME 2

Spider, Kitty, Voodoo, Whatever It Takes, The Camp, Lorry, Magic, Haunted

JACKPOT MILLIONAIRE

Danny Taylor is a middle-aged, working-class bloke who dreams of a better life away from the drudgery of work and his mundane, repetitive existence. He fantasises about being rich and having fast cars and even faster women. All this could become a reality if only he could win the lottery. Would this really lead to the fantastic life he imagines?

Jackpot Millionaire is a hilarious, fast paced comedy.

THE RAVEN'S VENGEANCE

The first Teagan O'Riordan mystery.

Events from the past spawn great vengeance in the sleepy Irish village of Rathkilleen. To catch a killer Detective Teagan O'Riordan will have to discover the secret of the Raven.

THE ANGEL OF DEATH

Devil worshippers bring sacrilege and death to Rathkilleen. Teagan has to unravel satanic rituals and demonic symbols in order to unmask the Angel of Death.

SHEER HATE

The Vigil is a vicious online newspaper that revels in muckraking and delights in ruining lives, leaving a trail of victims in its wake with deadly consequences. Seductive reporter, Silky Stevens, and sleazy photographer, Frank Ebdon, will do anything to get a front-page story. Journalist, Nick Rose, struggles with his past, but is forced to use all his investigative skills to unmask a killer driven by sheer hate.

Printed in Great Britain
by Amazon

44726056R00118